THE C AGREEMENT

A RENDEZVOUS NOVEL

R.L. KENDERSON

THE C AGREEMENT

AUTHOR NOTE
CONTENT WARNING

The heroine is plus-size, and while she is comfortable with her body there are fat women realities mentioned. There is also light bondage, orgasm play, a good girl kink, and the hero likes to be in control in the bedroom.

ONE
RAYNE

WITH A HEAVY SIGH, I DROPPED INTO THE RESTAURANT booth and let myself finally relax.

"Bad day?" my sister-in-law, Em, asked as she dipped her tortilla chip into the salsa.

Sliding toward the wall, I said, "Not exactly bad. Just long. It felt like it dragged even though I was busy. I'm glad to be done with work for the weekend. How about you two?"

"Same," Beau said. "I'm glad it's Friday and that we're having Mexican."

"Hear, hear," Em said and clinked her margarita glass against my brother's beer.

"The whole week was long," I said, picking up a chip for myself.

The only day that hadn't felt like it was doubled in time was the day I met up with Vivian and Delaney for our Women in Law program. We went to high schools across the Minneapolis area to tell young women about what it was like to be female lawyers. And the three of us were really getting our groove down for when we did our presentations. Plus, I had made a couple of new friends out of the whole thing.

Em gasped. "Oh my God, Rayne, I forgot to ask. How was your weekend getaway? I kept meaning to message you and ask, but then I figured I would find out all the details once I saw you again." She chuckled.

A warm body slid in next to me.

"What weekend getaway?" Cade Nichols, my brother's best friend, asked.

I didn't want to talk about Brett. "Never m—"

"Rayne went on a romantic trip with Brett," Em answered.

"Who's Brett?" Cade asked.

I turned to him, my jaw dropping. "Do you pay attention to anything about me?"

He grinned, and I noticed how his wavy brown hair was messy, likely from him running his hands through it all day. His black button-up shirt and black pants were wrinkled from being at work for eight hours. And yet he still looked like he'd stepped out of a men's magazine. Even though I was a woman and he was a man, I used to be jealous of how he always looked good. Especially with his deep blue eyes and that cocky smile he'd perfected over the years.

"Only the good stuff."

My brother and Cade were two years older than me,

and my sister-in-law had been in the year between us in school. Beau and Em were high school sweethearts, and since Cade didn't date women seriously and I was the fat, younger sister that my brother could bring with him so Cade had someone to talk to and so our parents would let him stay out later, the four of us had hung out a lot. Now that we were adults, we tried to get together at least once a month for dinner, so he should have known who my ex-boyfriend was.

"Brett and I dated for over a year," I pointed out.

Cade lifted a shoulder. "You should have brought him out to eat with us."

"I did. I brought him several times."

Cade rubbed his chin. "I guess he wasn't important enough for me to remember."

I opened my mouth to come up with something to refresh his memory until I remembered that I didn't want to think about or talk about Brett anymore, and I clamped my mouth shut. Why I fought so hard for things I didn't even care about, I didn't understand sometimes.

"Rayne," Em said, her brow furrowed in confusion, "did you say, 'dated for over a year'?"

My brother picked up his beer and looked at his wife. "I don't get it."

"She didn't say, *We've been dating for over a year*. She said they *dated* for over a year. Past tense."

"We broke up," I said as quickly as I could while I leaned over Cade to catch the nearest server's attention. "Yes, hi. Can I get a margarita? Please. Unless you're not

3

our server, and in that case, can you please tell whoever is our server that we're in desperate need of a drink?"

The woman laughed. "You're in luck. I am your server."

I sighed. "God bless you."

She turned from me to Cade. "And you, sir?"

"I'll have a beer. And a paddle to smack this ass in my lap."

Immediately, I flew back in my seat and elbowed him as I pushed my long blonde hair over my shoulder. "Jerk."

I had been so fixated on ending any conversation that had to do with why Brett and I had broken up that I didn't pay attention to what I was doing.

He laughed and squeezed my knee. "Relax, Storm. It's a nice butt."

Around middle school, Beau and Cade had given me the nickname Rayne Storm when I was mad. Over the years, it had shrunk from Rayne Storm to Storm, and the two men still liked to use it when I got heated, which thankfully didn't happen as often as it had when I was a kid.

I pushed his hand away. "Ha-ha. You're so funny," I said sarcastically.

"I'm not—"

"Hey," my brother said from across the table and pointed a finger at Cade. "No hitting on my sister."

I rolled my eyes. There were so many reasons that would never happen. My brother didn't have anything to worry about.

4

"Is there anything else I can get the table?" our server asked. "Are you ready to order?"

"I'm ready," Em said and looked at Cade and me. "Are you two?"

This particular restaurant was one of our favorites, and all four of us had the menu memorized.

"I know what I want," Cade said.

I nodded. "Me too."

The server went around the table, taking our orders.

After she left, Em said, "I'm glad to see you're eating normally again."

I frowned, confused, until I realized what she was referring to. "Oh, yeah, I had a moment of weakness, but that was a while ago."

"I know. But since it seems like you and Brett broke up, I can say, I was worried for a second there."

Over the past couple of years, I had worked really hard to love my body the way it was. I read tons of books on weight and health, subscribed to podcasts discussing the same things, and even read some medical journal articles.

I had learned a lot about how weight and health did not equate to the same thing, but it was hard when we lived in such a skinny-focused world. And there were so many people who looked at me and assumed I was lazy and overweight when, in reality, I worked out regularly, ate healthy during most meals, and always had good lab result numbers when I went to the doctor.

But even after all that, it was hard to get over all the

fatphobia I'd learned, growing up, and sometimes, I fell back into old habits.

Like when I'd thought maybe my boyfriend was no longer interested in me because I had put on a few pounds. I was mad at myself for even thinking I wasn't worth sleeping with because of my size, especially because if Brett had really thought that, it would have been time for him to go, not time for me to try another diet that wouldn't work.

Turned out, that hadn't been the problem at all. And I still couldn't figure out if the real reason he had slowly withdrawn from our sex life was better or worse. Probably worse.

"What's this now about you not eating?" Cade said, his brow furrowed.

Em knew how much work I'd done on myself, and my brother knew some of it, but Cade didn't really know much. It wasn't something gorgeous, muscular men who simply looked at a treadmill and lost weight would ever understand even if I knew he'd be supportive.

"Nothing." I wiggled the chip in my hand that I had already picked up. "I'm eating."

"Good, because you don't need to starve yourself for some asshole." His voice was firm.

I put my hand on his arm. "I'm not starving myself for anyone." Not even myself. I looked at my sister-in-law. "Brett and I are done, and even if he wanted to get back together, I wouldn't. So, please, don't worry about me."

Just worry about my sex life instead.

TWO

RAYNE

Our plates were cleared, and another round of drinks was brought to our booth. As our server walked away, Cade's phone buzzed against the table, and the screen lit up.

I was too far away to read what it said, but my brother looked at it and frowned.

"I see you're planning to leave us soon," he said to his best friend.

"Not soon." Cade shrugged. "But I have plans for when this dinner is over."

"Yeah, 'plans,' " Beau said with air quotes. "He's leaving us to have sex."

I took a drink of my margarita and smirked. "You sound jealous," I teased my brother.

"I am."

Em's jaw dropped.

"I barely get to see the guy, and he's going to leave me

to get laid," my brother added before his wife could yell at him.

My sister-in-law put her hand on her chest. "You scared me for a second there."

Beau threw his arm around her. "Em, you know I don't want to have meaningless sex with a bunch of strangers. I only want to be with you."

"She's not a stranger," Cade protested.

We all turned our eyes to him with eyebrows raised.

While my brother was a one-woman man—Em and Beau had been together since high school after all—Cade was the opposite. In all the years I'd known him, he'd never gotten serious with anyone. He blamed his parents' failed marriage, which probably did factor into his permanent single status, but it probably didn't hurt that he was attractive and got his fair share of women. If I was sexy and gorgeous, I would probably play the field more myself instead of dating the first guy who showed interest after each failed relationship.

Cade gestured toward his phone. "She literally sent me a text; therefore, she can't be a stranger."

"Yeah, because hookup sites don't exist," my brother said mockingly. "Just because she has your phone number doesn't mean you've met her yet."

"I've met her."

"So, what is she then?" I asked.

Cade sighed. "She's one of my regulars," he admitted.

It was my turn for my mouth to fall open. "You have regulars?"

"Yes. I have a certain number of women I can call up when I want to have sex. We have a mutual understanding that it's a *scratch my back, I scratch your back* kind of thing."

"But that's only when he can't find someone to take home from the bar or club," Beau said.

"Or if I don't feel like going out," Cade added.

"Wow," I said.

I had seen him in action. He was tall, muscular, and handsome. All he had to do was give his *aw-shucks* smile, and women were ready to go home with him. And yet that wasn't enough for him. He had *regulars*.

Cade fell back against the bench seat. "I like sex, okay?"

I wished I'd liked sex that much.

My brother took a sip of his beer and smiled. "I bet—"

Em and I groaned loudly, but Beau and Cade ignored us. The two of them had been betting and daring each other to do things since middle school.

"I bet," my brother started again, "that you can't abstain from sex for a whole month."

My eyes darted over to Cade.

He laughed and shook his head. "You're right; I can't. I'm not betting on that."

Beau leaned forward. "What if I made it worth your while?"

Sometimes, their bets were just to prove to the other that they could do it, but other times, they put up cash or other items of interest as the prize.

Cade lifted his beer to his mouth. "I don't know, man. Unless you're going to give me a million dollars, I don't think it's worth it. You know how much I like sex. You know how much I *have* sex. I mean, would you go a month without getting laid?" he asked Beau, glancing at Em to drive his point home. "What about you? Would you go a month without sex?"

Beau narrowed his eyes in thought as he looked at his wife before turning back to his friend. "Okay, that's fair. I don't even like going a week—"

Em snorted. "A week? How about two days?"

Beau picked up her hand and kissed the back of it, but he didn't take his eyes off Cade.

"I don't like going a week, so how about this?" Beau smiled almost sinfully. "If you can have sex with the same person for one month, starting tonight, I will open Blaze with you." He checked his watch. "It's the third, and March has thirty-one days, so the bet would end on April third. Do you think you can handle that?"

Cade hissed, and I sucked in a deep breath.

My brother was the head chef at a popular restaurant in St. Paul, and Cade was a world-class bartender and manager at another high-end restaurant in Minneapolis. Cade had been asking my brother to start up their own restaurant together for years. He was so determined that he'd even named their place Blaze, but Beau almost always told him no. Occasionally, he'd get a *maybe someday in the future*.

To say I was shocked that my brother would offer Blaze as a prize was an understatement.

And apparently, Em thought the same thing because she said, "Excuse me, shouldn't we talk about this?"

Beau looked at his wife. "You're always telling me it's a good idea and that I'd get to make the recipes that I want to make if I had my own place."

"I know, but I wasn't prepared for you to suddenly change your mind like this."

He shrugged. "Cade has to agree to it *and* win the bet, so it might not even happen."

"But how would he prove it?" I asked.

"Great question," Em added.

Beau shrugged. "I trust him to tell me the truth." He looked at his friend. "You wouldn't lie when it involves something as important as our careers or futures, right?"

"No, I wouldn't." This was the first thing Cade had said since my brother had brought up the restaurant, but I couldn't figure out what he was thinking. His face was stoic.

Beau smiled. "Good enough for me."

"Still, you should talk to the woman he chooses to sleep with to see how many nights they're together or something," Em said. "I know it wouldn't mean he didn't sleep with someone else, but it would make it less likely."

My brother rubbed his chin. "That is a thought. But we have to see if Cade agrees or not." He smiled. "I'm heading to the restroom. I'll give you a minute to think."

"I'll go with you," Em said and slid out of the booth behind my brother.

When it was the two of us, I asked, "Do you want me to leave too?"

"No."

I turned in my seat to face him. "Do you want to talk about it? You haven't said much."

Cade's brow furrowed. "I think I'm in shock. I never thought Beau would give Blaze a chance, much less base his decision on a bet."

"Maybe because he thinks you'll say no or he doesn't think you can do it."

Cade's jaw tightened.

"*Or* maybe he wants to do it, but he can't quite say yes, and you winning this bet will be the push he needs," I offered.

"Maybe," Cade said as if he knew I had only said that to make him feel better.

"Are you more bothered that he might think you can't do it or that you won't get to sleep with multiple women?"

He scowled at me. "The former. But also, I don't sleep around because I need a new woman in bed every night. If I sleep with the same woman all the time, she's going to get the wrong idea and think I want a commitment." He looked away. "That, and a few other reasons."

Too bad Cade didn't have someone he trusted not to fall in love with him after a month of being together. He needed someone like me, who had known him forever and saw him as a friend. Who also wouldn't mind having sex with him.

I eyed him up and down. I definitely wouldn't mind getting naked with Cade. With his repertoire, he could probably teach me a thing or two.

I gasped. "Oh my God."

"What?" he asked.

"I know how badly you want Blaze to happen, but are you willing to go through with the bet?" I laughed at the thought forming in my head. "Because I have an idea."

THREE
CADE

My eyes fell to Rayne's plump lip as she chewed on it. I could almost see the wheels turning behind her brown eyes, and I couldn't help but smile.

"What's your idea?" I asked. I couldn't wait to see what she was concocting in her cute head.

Beau dangling our restaurant in front of me was definitely the most tempting thing he could have offered for me to agree to this bet of his. The only problem was, I had no desire to settle down with anyone, and the thought of picking one woman to screw for a month almost made my dick shrivel up. Almost. The reason I had multiple regulars was because I liked to fuck. A lot. I didn't want anyone to get too attached to me, which was why I spread repeat visits out. And sleeping with someone regularly for thirty-one days might give them the wrong idea. But the alternative sounded worse. Going a whole month with zero sex sounded like torture.

So, if Rayne had an idea of how I could win this bet without getting tied down with someone, I was all ears.

She looked down at herself, then back up to me. "Never mind," she said with a chuckle. "It was a silly thought."

She started to face forward again, but I stopped her with a hand on her knee.

"I doubt that." I rubbed my thumb over her smooth skin. "Tell me. Let me decide if it's silly."

She arched her neck and looked around before relaxing back in her seat. "If I tell you this, it stays between the two of us, okay?"

My eyebrows flew up. While I considered Rayne a friend, she was my best friend's little sister first, and I didn't think we'd ever had a secret that we kept from Beau. Or Em for that matter.

"It doesn't concern my brother or Em, but it is embarrassing, which is why I don't want anyone to know," she added when I didn't answer her.

I nodded. "Your secret is safe with me."

Rayne opened her mouth, paused, grabbed her margarita, and downed the rest.

I chuckled. "Liquid courage?"

"Yeah, something like that."

Rubbing my thumb on her knee, I said, "Take your time."

"Can't. Beau and Em will be back soon, and I absolutely do *not* want my brother to hear this." She sucked in a big breath and then exhaled.

"Rayne, it can't be that—"

"I suck in bed," she blurted out.

What?

"What?"

"Really? You're going to make me say it again?"

I shook my head. I'd heard her the first time. "I guess I don't understand."

Breaking eye contact, she muttered, "Brett and I broke up because he said that he would rather fuck a dead fish than me." Her cheeks turned bright red.

My body was also heating up, but for an entirely different reason. "*What the fuck?*"

Rayne jumped as her eyes flew back to mine. "Shh...I don't need anyone to know about this. I haven't even told any of my friends." Dropping her head in her hands, she said, "It's so humiliating."

I tugged on her wrists. "No, it's not."

She shot me a *don't be ridiculous* look. "If I were eighteen, sure, but I'm almost thirty. I should know what I'm doing in bed."

Not if she'd had lousy-ass lovers.

But saying that out loud wasn't going to lessen her embarrassment, so I just told her the truth. "What an asshole."

"Yes. But also, no."

"There is no *no* about it."

She lifted a shoulder. "If he hadn't told me, then I wouldn't have known I needed to fix it."

I ground my teeth together. One person's opinion didn't make it fact.

"But that's where my idea comes in."

"What idea?"

She chuckled, and I was happy to see something other than despair on her face.

"My idea. For the bet."

My brow furrowed. "What does one have to do with the other?"

Oh shit.

Don't say it.

Please don't say—

"I'll have sex with you for the month—no strings attached—and in turn, you can help me become a better lover."

She said it.

She bit her lip again when I didn't say anything. "What do you think? You'll get your restaurant, and I'll get better in bed."

"No."

RAYNE

I frowned. "No? What do you mean, no?"

I thought it seemed like the perfect plan, but then he eyed me up and down, assessing me.

And it clicked.

"I get it." I felt the heat rise to my cheeks once again.

How many times did I have to be mortified in one night? Make that, in the last ten minutes.

He snorted. "You do?"

"Yeah." And because I was a little pissed off that he wouldn't even consider my idea, I decided to put him on the spot. It was only fair that he felt awkward too. "You're not into fat chicks."

I had done a lot of work on myself and my body, and I'd come to find parts of myself that were attractive. But I sometimes forgot that everyone else in my life still lived by societal standards, and looking back, I had never seen Cade with a fat woman before. Thicker women? Sure. Voluptuous women? Definitely. Fat? No.

He scowled and slowly turned toward me. "What the fuck did you say?" he growled through clenched teeth.

Whoa.

I swallowed. I didn't see him mad a lot, and I didn't know what to do. "Uh..." My eyes darted around before coming back to him. "You're not attracted to me." I shrugged, trying to show him it was okay even if I felt like a fool for offering myself up for sex. "It's not a big deal."

I slumped back in my seat, wishing Beau and Em would come back so this night could end. I wanted to pay my bill and get out of there. It looked like I was the only one who was going to feel any sort of embarrassment tonight because Cade was definitely not.

"Just please don't say anything to anyone," I whispered.

I suddenly pictured Cade telling his friends—minus my brother—about my proposition and them all laughing at the fat chick for even thinking she had a chance.

I didn't cry or feel sorry for myself a lot, but I could feel the unwelcome burning in the backs of my eyes. Just what I needed to complete my night.

"Get out," I demanded with a lift of my chin.

Cade was still staring at me, so I knew he'd heard me.

"Rayne." His jaw was hard, and he had the audacity to look mad at me.

I grabbed my purse. "Get. Out." I wished I were smaller, so I could climb over him to get out of the booth, but even attempting it would just remind us both why he had turned me down.

"I'm not moving until we talk."

Is he serious? I had lived twenty-nine years, having guys explain to me that they saw me as just a friend. Or that I had a pretty face, but they didn't like me that way. He didn't need to feed me all his bullshit. I'd been hearing it my whole life.

I got in his face until we were nose to nose. "Get the fuck out of my way before I scream."

His eyes narrowed, but surprisingly, he turned away and got out of the booth.

I scrambled out before he could change his mind. "Tell my brother I'll send him some money for dinner," I said over my shoulder and bolted out of the restaurant.

I hoped Cade lost the fucking bet.

FOUR
RAYNE

I WAS NURSING MY THIRD GLASS OF WINE AND ignoring texts from Beau and Em. I didn't want to talk to anyone right now. Pretending like tonight had never happened seemed like a better use of my time.

I snorted into my glass. That wasn't possible. At least, not for a long time.

There was a knock at my door, and my eyes flew up to the clock on my wall. It was after eleven. Too late for house calls.

My phone buzzed again, and I sighed.

I loved my brother, but he could be overprotective.

Dragging my feet to the door, I looked out the side window. I frowned at what I saw there.

I flipped the dead bolt and yanked the thick wood open. Cade stood there in a ribbed tank top, looking as handsome as ever, with muscular arms on display and his jeans showing off his perfect denim-covered ass. I didn't need to actually see it tonight to know how great it looked. Meanwhile, I was in light-pink-and-soft white pajamas. I probably looked like a marshmallow while he looked like he was ready for a magazine cover.

"What are you doing here?" I said with a sigh. "Come to humiliate me more?"

His brow furrowed. "What the fuck, Rayne? No."

Okay, so Cade had never done anything to purposely demean me, and I probably wasn't being fair to him. My feelings had been hurt, and I had lashed out at him. Although he could have let me down a little gentler.

My shoulders slumped. I was tired. "I'm sorry I said that. It was uncalled for." I rubbed my temples. "It's late. Can we do this tomorrow?" *Next week? Never?*

He stepped closer and pulled my wrist down. "No. Not until you let me—"

Yanking my hand away, I slammed the door in his face before he could finish his sentence.

Not until you let me apologize, was what I was sure he was going to say.

The last thing I wanted was for him to feel sorry for me. That would almost be worse than a straight-out rejection.

Before I could secure the lock, the door swung open again. I jumped back before I got hit in the face, and my jaw dropped as Cade marched inside.

He kicked it closed, grabbed me, and hauled me up against the wood. One arm was on my waist and the other next to me, effectively blocking me in. I felt every inch of his body heat, and his eyes burned with fury as he stared down at me.

"You just can't let me say what I came to say, can you?"

I opened my mouth, but only a squeak came out.

I wasn't afraid. It was just that I had never seen Cade like this—besides the small glimpse I'd gotten at the restaurant. He was my older brother's fun, laid-back friend who never took life too seriously. Blaze was the thing he was the most passionate about, so I had no idea where this side of him had come from.

"You don't need to exp—"

I was stopped by the hand on my hip wrapping around my throat. It wasn't tight, but it sent a message.

"Shut up," he growled.

That was the one.

My breath caught, and there was a flood in my panties. "Holy—"

He squeezed.

I might have whimpered.

"I said, shut up." His eyebrows rose, as if he couldn't believe I was still talking.

I nodded as I squeezed my legs together. This was a side of Cade I would have never thought existed.

He dropped his head toward my ear. "I can't believe you think so little of me. You've known me forever, so you should know I'm not a shallow, judgmental person, Rayne."

I closed my eyes. He was right. Even though I had never seen him with a fat woman before, Cade had this quality that gave the impression that he saw the beauty in everyone. Which was probably why I had been bold enough to offer for us to help each other out in the first place.

"I am attracted to women. All types. Their smell, their taste, their skin, their breasts, their everything." He rubbed his nose along my jaw. "Your skin...it's soft and creamy. You smell delicious."

His words...his words were everything, and instinctively, I jerked my hips forward, searching.

And when his hard cock grazed against my clit, I moaned.

"Jesus," he muttered.

He backed up just enough to slam his mouth over mine.

Cade's tongue swept into my mouth as he thrust his pelvis into mine. His dick was long and thick, and I completely forgot that I'd been told I was bad in bed. I wanted to feel him inside me.

All too soon, he jerked his head back and met my eyes. "I find you sexy as fuck, but you're my best friend's little sister. Completely off-limits. So, I've never allowed myself to think of you that way, and that is why I told you no."

My chest heaved as I stared up at him.

He tipped his head down. "Understood?"

I nodded, as if in a daze. I couldn't believe this gorgeous man, who could get almost any woman he wanted, thought I was sexy. And that he'd kissed me like that.

The corners of his eyes crinkled. "Good. Now, the only thing I want you to say is, *I'm sorry.*"

He loosened his hand but kept it on my throat as his thumb caressed my pulse.

I licked my lips. "I'm sorry."

He smiled. "Good girl."

My knees buckled.

"*Fuck,*" he murmured as his eyes heated.

He looked down, as if contemplating something, and then back up at me.

"Do you come, Rayne?"

I gulped, not expecting that question. "Wh-what?"

He grinned. "Do you come?"

I lifted a shoulder. "Yes." I had a whole drawer full of vibrators that helped me come all the time.

"Let me be more specific. Have you come when you're with your partners?"

I looked away, ashamed.

"Eyes on me." His voice was firm yet soft.

My gaze immediately returned to his. "I suck in bed, remember?" I said in a low voice.

His eyes roamed my face. "Somehow, I doubt that. Now, tell me, have you ever had an orgasm with any of your partners?"

"I've had one or two during oral sex, but not from *sex,* sex."

His jaw tightened. "I suspect it's not you who has the problem in bed."

"I don't know. I am the common denominator in all my relationships."

"That doesn't mean shit."

He pushed his pelvis into me again.

"Are you wet?"

"Embarrassingly so," I admitted.

I couldn't believe I'd just thrown that out there. It was like I couldn't *not* answer him.

The hand around my neck trailed down my chest and over my beaded nipple. Cade pinched it before moving to the other side, where he flicked it with a finger. The almost roughness of his actions made me flinch, but only in surprise and not in a bad way. No, the fact that they made my core clench said it was very good.

His hand continued south until his fingertips slipped underneath my pajama bottoms and then my underwear.

He paused for a moment, maybe to see if I would stop him, but when I didn't, his whole hand disappeared into the cotton, and a finger brushed my cleft.

"Open."

He didn't have to tell me twice, and as soon as I widened my legs, he circled my clit and pushed two long digits inside me.

"Fuck me," he groaned. "You are soaked."

I was about to tell him I had warned him, but he curled his fingers and rubbed that sweet spot inside of me that I only seemed to be able to find half the time with my various sex toys. And yet he had found it right away.

I knew he would be an excellent teacher in the bedroom.

Soon, I was rotating my hips as he worked his hand between my legs.

His mouth was near my ear again. "There's another reason I said no earlier tonight, Rayne."

"What's that?" I managed to say between my deep breaths. Trying to pay attention to what he was saying and my impending orgasm was torture.

"I like to be in control. No, I *need* to be in control. Not always, but most of the time. And if you were going to be the only woman I fucked, I didn't want to put that on you for an entire month. I know how strong you are. How hard-headed you are sometimes."

With every sentence, he continued to stroke me.

"But seeing you tonight, here against your door, letting me wrap my hand around your beautiful neck, listening to my commands"—he chuckled—"in the end anyway—and letting me put my hand between your sweet thighs, I think you might be able to handle me."

My fingers were already buried in his tank. I twisted the material in my hands at his words.

"Do you think you can handle me, Rayne?" He licked my neck and sucked on my overheated skin.

I nodded.

"Let's see, shall we?"

What does that mean?

Cade swept his thumb over my clit and pushed down.

"Come for me, Rayne. Right the fuck now."

He bit down on my neck, and lightning exploded in my body, starting from my center and spreading to every single cell. I had to seize his shoulders so that I didn't melt into a puddle on the floor.

When I finally blinked my eyes open, Cade was staring at me, and his hand was still buried between my legs.

He slowly withdrew his fingers from my body, and I instantly missed his touch.

My entryway light was on from when I'd answered the door, and he held his hand up in the light.

His fingers were glossy and shiny from my desire.

Cade shoved his middle finger in his mouth as he closed his eyes and dragged it out as his cheeks hollowed. His lids flipped open, and his blue eyes met my gaze. "Open. I want you to see how good you taste."

Without even a second thought, I let my lower jaw drop, and Cade smiled as he pushed his ring finger inside.

"Suck."

Again, I did as he'd said even though I didn't know if I really wanted to know what I tasted like.

He slowly withdrew his digit from my mouth, as if he wanted to make sure I licked everything clean, so right before his finger was free, I ran my tongue around the tip.

"You're going to fucking kill me, Rayne."

I frowned. "What do you mean?" I asked.

He stepped back and removed his wallet from his back pocket. He pulled out a card and shoved it into my hand.

"Meet me there. Tomorrow. They open at ten."

He drew me away from the door and opened it as I looked down at the scrap of paper in my hand.

It was for a clinic.

Cade strode outside, leaving me confused.

"Wait."

He spun around.

I waved the card. "What does this mean?"

"It means, you and me for the next month. No one else for me." He tilted his head down. "And no one else for you."

I gasped as I realized he was going to take me up on my idea.

"But what does the clinic have to do with it?"

"If I'm only going to be fucking you for the next month, I don't want *anything* between us."

My eyes went wide.

"You on the pill?"

"Yeah."

He gave me his cocky smile. "Good." He skipped down my two steps and headed for his SUV.

"But what made you change your mind?"

I held my breath because if he was doing it to prove I had been wrong earlier tonight or because he felt sorry for me, then I was going to tell him no.

He turned once more and walked backward.

"Because you were a very good girl."

FIVE
CADE

I started my SUV, and as I waited for my phone to connect, I brought my fingers to my nose and inhaled.

If someone had told me that my best friend's little sister had the best-smelling pussy in the world, I wouldn't have believed them. Yet the proof was literally in my hands.

Or rather, on my hand.

Whatever.

I couldn't wait to strip off her panties and shove my tongue in her cunt.

Because I had been around a lot of pussies, and from what I could tell, hers was by far the finest out there.

I put my vehicle in reverse and pulled out of Rayne's driveway, wondering what I had gotten myself into.

After the disaster at dinner, I had canceled my "date" for the night, and I tried to stay away from Rayne and give her time to cool down. *I* needed to give myself a chance to cool down.

But after several hours with my blood pressure still through the roof, I threw on some clothes and drove over to her house. I had considered messaging or calling her, but after the way she hadn't let me speak at the restaurant, I figured I might as well not waste time since she was probably going to ignore me.

I only planned to tell her that she was wrong in her assumption of me, but as I drove over, I couldn't stop thinking about what she had confessed to me. Her ex-boyfriend telling her she was bad in bed definitely hadn't helped her self-esteem when it came to her body, and if I didn't help her, who would?

Nobody?

Some asshole who only wanted to take advantage of her?

The farther I drove, the more I considered helping her. And while I might have to set aside some of my sexual needs for the next month, this way, I would still be able to have sex, and I would get to open Blaze, like I'd been wanting to do for years.

I had gone over there with the best intentions. Or at least, semi-good ones.

But I had been upset and horny, and when she wouldn't let me say what I needed to say, I'd instinctively reached out and put my hand around her throat.

I'd known Rayne since she was young, and I knew how strong of a person she was. She had put up with a lot of bullying during her school years, yet she had graduated with great grades and gone to college, then law school. I had fully expected her to drop-kick me when I touched her. But it appeared Rayne had a good-girl complex.

And I loved me a good girl.

"Fuck," I grumbled and hit Beau's name on my speed dial.

"Hello?" his groggy voice answered.

I glanced at the clock. It was almost midnight.

Shit.

"Sorry, man. I lost track of time."

"It's fine. No work tomorrow. What's up?"

"I thought about your bet."

I hadn't given an answer because Rayne had taken off just as Beau and Em were coming back to the table. And since I'd promised not to tell them Rayne's reason for her relationship ending, I couldn't tell them anything that had happened after she confessed that her ex told her she was bad in bed.

Not that I would ever tell my best friend that his little sister had offered to be my fuck buddy for the next month so that not only could I win the bet, but so that she'd be a hot lay too.

Yeah. That wasn't ever going to fucking happen.

So, I had made up some bullshit, saying that Rayne suddenly had to go, and went to pay the bill. Then, I had gotten out of there before Beau could ask any more questions about his sister or what she had said to me before leaving. I could string some bullshit along when it helped with my job, but not when it came to my best friend. He knew me too well and for far too long.

Beau chuckled. "Since it sounds like you're driving, I'm going to go with, you're not going to take me up on the bet. Or you already lost."

I shot the phone a scathing look, as if it were my actual friend. "Neither, shithead. And, Jesus Christ, I haven't done two chicks in one night in years."

"Is that because you're old or because your dick is starting to shrivel up from too much use and abuse?"

"If my dick is shriveled, so is yours since you can't seem to keep it out of your wife."

"Do you blame me?"

"Do you really want me to answer that?"

Beau laughed again. "No."

"That's what I thought."

"Okay, so you called to say, you do want to go through with the bet?"

"Sure as hell do."

He made a noise that sounded like he was sucking air through his teeth.

"Having second thoughts?" I asked. "Rayne thinks you made this bet with me so that if I win, you'll be forced to open our restaurant. That it'll give you the push you need to go through with it."

"Did she, huh?"

"Or that you think I can't do it, and then you'll have a reason to get me off your back." It wasn't exactly what she had said, but it was close enough.

"So, who's the lucky lady?"

"Huh?"

"Fucking Rayne."

I froze because, unless Beau had cameras secretly installed at his sister's house, there was no way he could possibly know what had just happened. I highly doubted she'd told him I'd stuck my hand down her pants and made her come all over my fingers.

I swallowed hard. "What?" I managed to say.

"Fucking Rayne," he repeated. "She's too smart sometimes."

Realizing that Beau had jumped back to what his sister had said to me about him, I breathed a sigh of relief.

I heard a shuffle, as if he was getting out of bed and walking. "She's right. Work has been...not so great lately. Every time I come up with a new menu idea, I get shot down by management. What's the point of being executive chef if I don't get to actually execute anything? I don't even get to cook as much anymore. Considering that alone, I would rather be the sous-chef."

"That's rough."

"Yeah. But I make good money, and I have health insurance. And with Em wanting to start a family—"

"What the fuck? You never said anything."

"Yeah, I know. We're not really telling anyone until we decide to start. Right now, it's just talk."

"Whoa," I said, sitting further back in my seat.

Once Beau and Em had a family, things were going to

change between us. And the restaurant would probably never happen.

"Anyway, I realized some things. Em also has a good job—one that can provide us with health insurance—and we don't have children yet. I'm thirty-one now, no longer a young kid in my twenties, and if we're going to do this, then the time is now."

I held my breath. Maybe I wouldn't even have to do the ridiculous bet. It almost sounded like he was ready to say yes tonight.

"So, now, all you have to do is win."

I huffed out a breath and rolled my eyes. "We could do this without the bet, you know."

"We could, but no. If you do this, it will show Em that you are serious about committing to our restaurant. She loves you like a brother, but she has her reservations." He laughed. "No pun intended."

I didn't laugh. "Are you sure you're not doing this just so I have to suffer?"

"That's just a bonus."

"You're an asshole."

"Maybe." He chuckled. "But you never answered me."

"About what?" I'd already forgotten the question.

"Who's the lucky lady? The one you had plans with tonight? Is she happy to be stuck with you for a month?"

I opened my mouth, ready to tell him no, but then I realized that I couldn't tell him who I was really going to have sex with.

"Yeah. Sure." I didn't know what else to say.

"Wow. You must like her."

"Something like that," I muttered.

"Hey, as long as it's not my fucking wife or sister, I don't care who you pick."

I winced. Beau had already warned me away from Rayne. The day she had turned eighteen, he'd told me that if I ever touched her, our friendship would be over. He didn't trust me not to hurt her.

But I wasn't going to hurt her. I was going to help her realize that she was better in bed than her lousy ex had led her to believe she was.

It didn't lessen the guilt eating away at me when I thought about breaking Beau's trust.

So, I did what any guy did when he didn't want to feel his feelings.

I made a joke.

"Not your wife or sister. Got it. Does this mean your mom's fair game?"

"Fuck you, asshole," Beau said with a laugh. "You wouldn't touch my mom if I paid you."

SIX

RAYNE

M͟y͟ ͟l͟e͟g͟ ͟b͟o͟u͟n͟c͟e͟d͟ ͟a͟s͟ I͟ ͟w͟a͟i͟t͟e͟d͟ ͟f͟o͟r͟ C͟a͟d͟e͟. I͟ ͟w͟a͟s͟ sitting alone on a bench at the front entrance of the clinic the next morning. It was early spring and normally still chilly outside, but it was a beautiful day. The sun was shining, and there was little wind. And I was too nervous to go inside to wait. There was a slight crisp in the air that reminded me I was about to do something that was going to change my relationship with Cade forever.

I had woken up early, even without my alarm clock, and couldn't think about anything else other than what had happened the night before and what was going to happen later today.

Before yesterday, I had planned on relaxing this morning, but instead, I had already cleaned my whole house and changed the sheets on my bed.

Just in case Cade really was planning to sleep with me.

Last night didn't seem quite real after waking up alcohol-free and with the light of day giving me a new perspective. And while I had gone to sleep, completely relaxed from the orgasm he'd given me, I realized that going any further could complicate our relationship irreparably.

And if my brother found out, it would complicate the relationship with him too. Not only for me, but also for Cade.

Sometime after I had turned eighteen, Beau had told me to stay far away from Cade. He said that Cade would only hurt me if I got involved with him. I was irritated at the time because I had gone to high school with Cade for two years and I had seen him with girls he'd dated. I knew he was a playboy, but it was as if my brother didn't think I was wise enough to pick up on that.

Besides, I had never shown interest in his best friend anyway. I already knew I eventually wanted to settle down someday after college and law school. I was smart enough to see that Cade was not the settling-down type.

And Cade had *never* shown an interest in me.

Until last night.

But, now, even though I was going into this thing with him for the next month with my eyes wide open and not expecting any strings attached, I didn't think Beau would give his blessing. I was a fully functioning adult, but he still saw me as the little sister he had to protect.

I saw movement out of the corner of my eye and recognized Cade's vehicle. I wasn't sure what I felt as I watched him park and get out of his SUV.

I was used to being comfortable around him. It was one

of the reasons I'd thought he'd be the perfect person to give me pointers.

But after seeing the other side of him yesterday evening, I was almost nervous. I didn't know what to expect or how to act.

I stood as he approached the entrance, and he grinned.

"Hey, Rayne. Early, per usual?" he teased.

It seemed he was back to the Cade I knew, so I replied, "Late, per usual?"

He laughed and grabbed my elbow. "Come on. They're waiting for us."

As I turned toward the front door, he put his hand on my back.

Him touching me was definitely new.

We made it to the desk to check in. It was a walk-in, same-day clinic, so I was surprised to find out we did have appointments for an STD check.

Once we were excused to find seats to wait, I asked him, "How did you get us in so fast?"

"I have connections."

"Right."

"I do. I know one of the nurses who works here. She got the two of us in today."

"Come here often?" I joked.

He shrugged. "I've come here enough. I want to make sure my partners are safe, and vice versa."

"Oh." I didn't know if I liked the fact that I wasn't the only one who had done this with him. "The nurse? Is she one of your regulars?"

He grinned. "Jealous?"

I groaned. "God, no." But maybe. A little.

"No. She's not. She's just a friend who helps me work the system. And they're connected to the hospital, which means they get their results fast."

"How fast?" I whispered.

"Within a couple of hours."

I slumped back into my chair.

"Did you think you had more time?"

"Yes, I guess I did."

"Well, I'm glad we don't. I canceled my plans last night, and I'm horny as hell. And feeling your tight, wet cunt as you came all over my hand didn't help. I don't know if I can even make it to the end of the day."

My mouth fell open. I had never had a boyfriend talk like that, especially in public.

I had to admit, it was hot.

"Please don't say any more," I said.

He frowned. "Why?"

"Because in a few minutes, someone's going to be looking at my vagina, and I don't need to be all wet."

He leaned back in his seat and grinned. "Rayne Thompson, I didn't know you talked like that."

"Why? Because I'm a woman?"

"No. Because you're Beau's little sister."

"Well, I'm not just his little sister. For the next month, I'm going to be your fuck buddy."

He put his arm around me and his mouth next to my

ear. "Not just my fuck buddy. You're also going to be my good girl."

I sucked in a sharp breath.

Why did those words do it for me?

I blamed romance novels.

But I still needed to make one thing clear.

I rubbed my cheek against his and whispered, "I'll be your good girl."

He groaned.

"But I won't be calling you Daddy."

Cade bellowed out a laugh as a voice called out my name to our left.

He removed his arm as he shook his head. "Go. Get checked out. After this, we're going to lunch."

I didn't know if that meant he was fine with me not calling him Daddy or if he was going to convince me to do it later.

SEVEN
RAYNE

We took our seats, adjacent to one another, at a corner table in the back of the restaurant and were given our menus, and as soon as the host left, Cade folded his hands on the table.

"I know I said I was going to move forward with this bet with you, but I think we need to discuss a few things before we come to an agreement."

"Okay," I said hesitantly.

His face was serious, and I was kind of nervous about what he had to say.

"Once we get the results back, I want you to know that I get you whenever and wherever I want you."

I swallowed hard. "You can't be serious."

"I am. You know how much I like sex. And if you're going to be my only partner, I need to know you're going to be available to me whenever I need you."

"But—"

He held up his hand, and I closed my mouth.

"I understand that you are doing me a favor—probably more than I am doing for you—but if I'm going to agree to this, I need full access to your pussy at all times."

My core clenched in arousal even if my mind was baffled at his speech.

He tilted his head. "In fact, you might as well start thinking of it as *my* pussy for the next thirty days. And if you're going to keep my pussy from me, I can't do this."

I had no words, but my panties were now soaked.

"There's a reason I have random hookups and a list of women I can call to sleep with, and it's not just because I like control. It's because I like sex. A lot. And if you're going to withhold it from me, then I can't do this. I'm not going to be fisting it several times a week because you're unavailable."

I licked my lips. Not only did I not want to lose the opportunity to see if sex with Cade could be as good as third base had been last night, but I also really wanted him to teach me to be a better lover. I wanted to give him what he had given me in the entryway of my house.

"What about work?"

He chuckled. "I'm not going to fuck you in front of your coworkers or anything like that."

When he said it out loud, I had to laugh.

"I'm sure you have a perfectly good restroom I can take you to, where I can bend you over." His brow furrowed, as if that gave him a thought. "You might need to wear only skirts to work from now on."

I couldn't tell if he was serious. My brother's best friend, Cade, was a jokester. But sexy Cade was a dirty talker who could make a sex worker blush.

"What about my period?"

"You get two days."

"Two days?" I squeaked. "But it usually lasts four."

"Is it bad all four?"

"Well…no."

"Then, you get two days." He tapped his pointer fingers together. "You said you were on the pill?"

"Yes."

"When you get to your fourth week, I want you to skip it and start your new pack. Then, you don't have to worry about your period."

"Don't you mean, you don't have to worry?"

He smirked. "I'm not the one who's worried."

He was right. He didn't seem to care. I did.

"Who are you?" I asked. I almost felt like I was having lunch with a stranger.

He threw his head back and laughed. Picking up my hand, he said, "Now, you see why I told you no."

"Hmm."

"Having second thoughts?"

Yes. "No." Not really anyway.

"You'll get used to me."

"If you say so."

"Never been with someone bossy in the bedroom?"

I had to give it serious consideration. "I definitely had some guys who liked to be in charge and others who would rather me be in charge, but nothing like you were last night."

"And what about you? Do you like to be in charge?"

That was an easy question. "No."

He grinned.

"But you already knew that."

"Not until last night." He squeezed my fingers. "But don't worry. I'll still teach you how to take initiative and what to do when you want something. You won't always have to wait for my commands."

My pussy clenched again at the word *commands*. Was I really into being bossed around? Apparently, I was.

"I appreciate that," I said because once this month was over, I was going to sleep with someone other than Cade. "But I just have one question."

"Shoot."

"What about your cock? Is it mine for a whole month?"

He licked his bottom lip and grinned. "Baby, it's yours whenever you want it."

"Even if you're not in the mood?"

He laughed. "I'm always in the mood for sex."

Knowing what I knew about him, even before the last two days, I knew he was telling the truth.

"And it goes without saying, you're the only one who is going to be in my bed this month."

I bit my lip. "I figured. Otherwise, this morning would have been a waste of time."

"I just needed to make it clear."

"I think it also goes without saying that we don't tell anyone about this," I said.

His eyes narrowed, which didn't make sense.

"Unless you want my brother to be pissed at the both of us."

His face relaxed. "Right. But I don't know if he'd be pissed at you. Probably just me."

"Let's not find out. And Em can't keep a secret from him, so it just stays between us."

"Right." Cade cleared his throat and shifted in his seat.

"Uh-oh. What's wrong?"

He looked surprised. "Who said anything was wrong?"

"You forget, I know you."

He looked into my eyes. "So then, you know this is a temporary thing, right, Rayne? You know I don't do relationships. I don't even sleep with the same woman twice in a row, much less the same one for a month at a time." He shuddered.

Tilting my head, I asked, "What about your regulars, as you call them?"

"I don't sleep with them in a row. I go weeks between seeing the same woman."

"Must be nice," I muttered.

"If you put it out there that you wanted to keep men on call for when you were horny, I'm sure you would find plenty."

Right. I was sure I could find some. Some who weren't picky about who they slept with. But I wasn't going to do that.

"Rayne?"

I lifted my head. I had zoned out for a second.

"Even if we have a good time together, it's best that we end things after a month. Less complications."

I shrugged and smiled. "I figured. I don't want to lie to Beau and Em forever."

"I'm serious. Don't fall in love with me, Rayne."

Wow. He was really worried I would get attached to him.

Leaning forward, I said, "I won't. It's just sex."

He frowned again.

"But you might want to make sure you don't fall in love with me," I said, my tone earnest.

He laughed, which was what I had been going for. He was worrying over nothing.

I took a deep breath. "So, we're really going to do this?"

His eyes narrowed, and he smiled. "I sure as hell hope so."

I smiled back. "We agree then. I'll be at your beck and call, and you'll teach me to be a rock star in the bedroom."

"That's too wordy. How about cock for cunt?"

"Ooh. Cock for cunt. It's a C agreement," I joked.

Cade's smile slowly melted as heat filled his eyes. His gaze shifted to a server headed our way, then back to me.

"As soon as we order our food, I want you to take that cunt into the restroom and take off your panties."

EIGHT

CADE

Rayne squirmed for the hundredth time as the server dropped off our bill and took our plates.

"Are you okay over there?" I asked, trying to hide my smile, already knowing the answer.

"No," she hissed. She leaned forward and dropped her voice. "You had me take off my underwear, but you haven't done anything about it."

It seemed we had different definitions of *doing anything about it.*

I cocked an eyebrow and smirked. "And what am I supposed to do?"

"I don't know. Touch me? Otherwise, what's the point?"

To build anticipation. I suspected most, if not all, of Rayne's past lovers hadn't taken much time with foreplay. And it was hard to be good in bed if one wasn't having that much fun.

"The point is, I know your pussy is bare under your pants." I smirked. "And it makes me happy." I picked up her hand and placed it on my crotch, where she could feel how hard I was. "Very happy."

She started to squeeze, and I quickly pulled her hand away. I'd been suffering just as much as she had throughout lunch. Her long blonde hair was up in a pony-tail today, and it was taking everything in me not to grab it and shove her head down so she could wrap her mouth around my aching length.

"You're no fun."

I laughed. "I'm very fun."

"Says you."

I loved how eager she was for me, but I was also surprised. After everything she'd told me last night about her ex and how embarrassed she was, I'd thought I was going to have to take things slow with her.

Although her impatience might be related to some-thing else that made sex feel less than fulfilling for her. She needed to stop and enjoy the moment.

"We have all day," I told her. "And we haven't gotten our results back yet." I pulled out my wallet and threw some money on the table. "Plus, I need to check on some things at work, and I'd like you to come with me."

She curled her upper lip. "Work? That really doesn't sound like fun."

I shrugged. "I understand. Especially if you have other plans."

She huffed out a breath. "You were my plans today."

I liked the sound of that.

She threw up her hands. "Why not? I'll go with you. I haven't been to your restaurant in forever."

It wasn't my restaurant, and that was the problem. I managed Iron House, but it would never be mine.

I stood. "We'll take your car to my place, and you can ride to Iron House with me."

Rayne got to her feet. "Does this mean I can put my underwear on?"

"No."

———

RAYNE

As soon as we walked into Iron House, the employees bombarded Cade. Since it was the middle of the afternoon, between the lunch crowd and the dinner crowd, there weren't many customers, but plenty of staff.

With each person approaching him with a problem, he calmly gave them instructions, answered their questions, or told them he'd look into it and get back to them.

Just like Friday night, this was a side of him I hadn't seen before.

I'd been to Iron House to eat maybe once in my life. The food was good but expensive, and in my opinion, I could get good food and spend much less money elsewhere. I made a decent income as an attorney for Hennepin County, but I wasn't rich.

With a hand on my back, Cade ushered me toward the beautiful oval-shaped hardwood bar that was centered in the middle of the restaurant. A woman looked up from the wineglass she was wiping and smiled.

"Sit here with Fallon for a few minutes. I need to go check on something in the kitchen. I'll be back."

"I'll be here," I said, but he was already walking away.

With a sigh, I pulled out the leather barstool and sat.

"He's busier than usual today," Fallon said, studying me.

"I noticed." I looked in the direction he'd gone even though I couldn't see him anymore. "I kind of wish I had turned down his invitation to come along. I'm probably in the way, and there are definitely things I could be doing at home." Like not thinking about sex.

"I haven't seen Cade bring women to the restaurant before. You must be special." She set the glass down. "Is there anything I can get you to drink?"

It was my turn to study Fallon. Was she curious or jealous? Or maybe she was simply making conversation with the stranger sitting in front of her because she was a bartender.

"Whatever is easiest for you," I told her.

She didn't need to go out of her way to cater to me.

She shrugged, pulled out a glass, and filled it with water.

After she slid it in front of me, I said, "I'm not special. I'm old friends with Cade. I'm Rayne, by the way."

"I don't know about not special. He's never brought a woman to work before."

My mouth dropped open, and I leaned forward. "*Never?*"

I knew he didn't get serious with anyone, but he did go on dates sometimes. Dates that never made it to a second one, but I'd figured he brought women here all the time to show off his place of employment.

Fallon shook her head. "Never."

I was surprised until I remembered who Cade was. "Well, I suppose he gets enough women here that he doesn't need to bring anyone in."

She shook her head again. "Nope. Anytime someone asks him out, he tells them no. He doesn't mix business with pleasure." She smiled. "Actually, he always says he doesn't shit where he eats."

Good for him. I hoped my brother realized how professional his best friend could be.

"Makes sense." I sipped on my water. "But seriously, I've known Cade since elementary school. My brother, Beau, is his best friend."

"Ohhhh." Fallon drew out the word. "Yeah, I know Beau." She tilted her head. "I can see the resemblance."

Beau and I both had blond hair and brown eyes, although his hair was slightly darker than mine. Beau, however, was average-sized, so people didn't always realize we were siblings.

"So, you've met my brother?"

"Yeah. He's come here a few times."

"Well, I'm the female version of Beau. Cade and I are just friends."

But did a friend stick their hand down their friend's pajamas and give them an orgasm?

Not that it mattered because the whole point of our agreement was that we *were* friends now and we would remain friends in the future.

"I believe you. I once heard him say that a woman who spends the night has been there too long."

"Yep, I've heard the same thing."

"So, has he ever had a girlfriend?"

I snorted. "Not as long as I've known him. I think he's allergic."

The two of us were laughing when Cade came around the bar. "What's so funny?"

"You," I told him.

Fallon's eyes got wide as she pursed her lips together like she was waiting to see what he would say next.

He lifted an eyebrow. "Do I want to know?"

"Nah."

"In that case, come back to the kitchen with me."

I slid off my stool. "Thanks for the water. It was nice meeting you," I said to Fallon and followed Cade.

"You're welcome," she said with a smile.

"I'm hoping we won't have to be here for too long," he said as he pushed the doors to the kitchen open. "But I do need to take care of a few more things before we can go."

"Whatever. If I want to leave, I'll just steal your car and go home."

He paused and waited for me to step up to him.

With his mouth next to my ear, he said, "And then I would have to spank your ass for taking something of mine home without my permission."

I leaned back so I could see his face. "I wouldn't keep your car, you know."

"I wasn't talking about my car." He glanced down at my crotch and back up to me as I sucked in a breath. "Come on. The chef wants me to try something."

His blatant remark about my vagina belonging to him, followed by something about work, played ping-pong in my brain, and I had to hurry to catch up with him.

I still didn't know how I felt about him claiming my pussy as his. I'd never had a boyfriend be possessive of my body in all the relationships I'd been in. And I was a strong feminist. No one owned me.

But fuck if it didn't turn me on.

The trickle of wetness between my legs reminded me that my underwear was still in my purse and that I needed to get my desire under control before it looked like I'd had a bathroom accident in my yoga pants.

When I reached him, his back was to me, and he was speaking to someone.

"Mmm, that is good." He spun around. "Open," he said with a lift of his chin as he held a spoonful of food in front of me.

I scanned the room to see a bunch of eyes on me.

When I turned back to Cade, the firm look in his eyes told me not to argue with him.

"Open, Rayne." His voice was deep and almost seductive.

Tentatively, I obeyed, and Cade carefully stuck the spoon in my mouth.

A rich garlic-and-cream flavor hit my tongue as I bit into the pasta. I was sure there were other flavors in there, but picking them out wasn't my strong suit. Quickly, I chewed the bite since it seemed like everyone was waiting to see what I thought.

Was tasting food always this serious in a kitchen?

I swallowed. "That was delicious."

Cheers erupted, and I jumped, surprised by how excited everyone was.

Cade grinned. "You made their day."

The kitchen staff turned their focus away from me and went back to doing their own things.

Smiling back, I threw my hands up. "I don't get it. They don't even know who I am."

"Chef Frank wanted someone who didn't work here to try his new dish, and I told him I knew just the woman to do it." He reached up and wiped the corner of my mouth. He held up his thumb and showed me the sauce that had been there. "Looks like I missed some."

I made sure no one was watching, and I grabbed Cade's hand to shove his thumb in my mouth. I wrapped my lips around the base, wanting him to picture me doing the same thing to his dick. As I slowly pulled his digit out, I sucked gently and nipped the tip.

I smiled innocently. "All clean."

He shook his head and tried to suppress a grin. "You're going to pay for that later."

NINE
CADE

I SHOWED RAYNE TO MY OFFICE, HOPING I WOULD BE done with work soon. I normally didn't have to come in on my days off, but both the owner and the weekend manager were out of town. Thankfully, Rayne liked to read and carried her e-reader in her purse, and I worked in a restaurant, so I had the kitchen make us a quick dinner.

By the time we left, I had kept her at Iron House for almost five hours. On the ride back to my house, she was silent, and I was feeling guilty.

"I'm sorry you had to wait for me for so long."

We had gotten our test results back several hours ago, giving us the all clear. The worst part was, I had planned to use the afternoon to tease her until she was ready to come from the slightest touch, but things hadn't gone the way I had wanted.

"I didn't mean to spend so long there."

She glanced away from the window. "It's fine. I know

work doesn't always go as planned." The smile she gave me didn't quite reach her eyes.

I didn't believe her that she was fine.

This was why I didn't do relationships.

When I wanted to fuck a woman, I did. No games. No wining and dining. And now, I had to smooth things over with Rayne if we were going to get naked tonight. And I really wanted to get naked with this woman. It had already been too long, and what had happened between us last night had me itching to see how good sex was between us.

It was a good thing this was Rayne, and she was worth a little extra effort.

Soon, we pulled into my garage, and I turned off my SUV. When she opened her door, I stopped her from getting out with a hand on her arm.

"Wait."

She turned in her seat to look at me and studied my face. "Oh no," she said, her shoulders sagging.

"Oh no? What's *oh no*?"

"You've changed your mind."

"What?" *Changed my mind? Not a chance.* "No."

Her eyes brightened. "You haven't?"

"Fuck no." I frowned. "Why would you think that?"

"Because you stopped me from getting out. Because you have such a serious look on your face. Because now that we're at your house, it seems more real."

I shook my head. "You have to stop thinking the worst all the time when it comes to the opposite sex."

"Well, to be fair, the last time a man looked at me like

you're looking at me, he told me he wanted to break up and that..." She cringed. "You know the rest."

I thought back to how she'd sucked my thumb in the restaurant kitchen, and it only added to my suspicion that Rayne had been with the wrong men.

It also got me hard again.

I picked up her hand and placed it on my erection. "I very much still want to do this."

She was staring at my lap when she licked her lips. "Me too."

"Jesus Christ," I muttered, imagining her sucking my cock like she had my thumb.

Her eyes jerked up to mine, and she tried to pull her hand away.

I didn't let her.

"What's wrong then? Why did you stop me from getting out?"

"You seemed...unhappy. I wanted to make sure you weren't upset with how our afternoon went. I know what women mean when they say, *It's fine*."

She leaned closer and used her free hand to cup my face. "When I told you it was fine, I meant it." She smiled. "Have I ever sugarcoated anything for you?"

I grinned. "No."

"And I'm not going to start now just because we're going to have sex." She dropped her arm. "I'm almost thirty. I don't have time for games."

Funny how she'd used that word.

"Then, what's wrong?" I tilted my chin down. "And

don't tell me nothing's wrong. I've known you for way too long."

She shook her head and rolled her eyes. "I'm nervous. I'm trying to tell myself not to be, but I can't help it."

"I would tell you not to be, but that's easier said than done. But know this: no matter what happens, it's going to be good." I squeezed her hand under mine to remind her how hard I was. "I can't wait to get inside you."

"Then, what are we sitting out here for?"

———

As soon as we were inside, I grabbed Rayne's hand and dragged her to my room.

I hadn't bothered to turn on any lights, but all my shades were still open, and streetlights guided my way.

Once we were in my bedroom. I let her hand go and quickly closed the curtains and turned on the lamp on my nightstand. I wanted to make her comfortable, but I also wanted to see her, and I figured the soft light of my lamp was better than the large overhead light on my ceiling fan.

Now, I just had to convince her that I was a safe person to get naked in front of.

But when I turned around, I discovered I didn't have to do anything because she had already removed her pants and sweater.

I stood frozen because, after last night, I'd thought she would be self-conscious about being nude. I was wrong.

She reached behind her to remove her black lace bra, knocking me out of my stupor.

"Don't you dare," I commanded. I needed more time to admire her creamy skin.

Her eyebrows flew up, but she immediately dropped her arms.

I couldn't believe this beautiful woman was mine to do what I wanted with for a whole month.

Maybe I needed to rethink my one-night-only hookups. Some of my regulars, who also didn't do commitment, might be open to spending a weekend together.

Although, when I tried to picture doing that with any of them, I couldn't think of a single one I wanted to be with for that long.

But I didn't need to worry about that for some time.

I ripped my shirt off, throwing it in the corner, and unzipped my jeans. I fisted my hand around my cock and pulled my aching length out.

"God, Cade," Rayne said breathlessly as she took me in.

"Rayne."

She shifted her gaze up.

I lifted my chin. "Be a good girl and continue. I want to watch."

She reached behind her again and unclasped her bra.

"Slowly," I muttered, stroking myself.

Rayne brushed her hands over her breasts and gradually up her shoulders until she reached the tops of them. With the same gentleness, she lowered the straps until they were wrapped around her biceps, her bra barely covering her.

I squeezed my dick. "Drop it."

She let the fabric fall to the floor, and I sucked in a breath upon seeing the deep red of her nipples. Rayne was pale and had never been a good tanner. Those two things, along with her blonde hair, had had me picturing them light pink. I couldn't wait to mark them with my teeth.

"On the bed. Lie on your back, knees up, and spread your legs."

Even though I was torturing myself by waiting to put my hands on her, it was necessary. I needed to see how well she followed directions, and I wanted her to practically climax by the time I touched her.

Again, she did exactly as I'd commanded, and when she bared her pussy to me, I let go of my hardness and dropped to my knees.

TEN
CADE

Starting at Rayne's ankles, I ran my hands up her legs, over her knees, and down her thighs as I stared at her cunt.

"What are you—"

"Shh..." My eyes flicked up to hers and back down. "You're going to let me look at my pussy. And when I'm ready, you're going to let me do what I want to it. To you."

Her outer lips were plump, but it was her inner lips that caught my attention. They were puffy and protruded out past her outer lips. I'd been with women who were self-conscious about their labias that were similar to this, but I loved it. To be fair, I loved every vagina I saw, but this kind was my favorite.

"I know I told you I would help you out in bed, but I need to take the edge off first. I promise I'm not going back on our deal, but I'm so horny that I can't even think right now."

I parted her, finding her swollen clit and her pink center, which was thankfully already wet.

But even so, Rayne hadn't said anything else.

"Do you understand? Is this okay with you?"

She nodded. "As long as you don't laugh at me."

I closed my eyes.

When I opened them, I told her, "I will never laugh at you." A slice of pain cut through my chest because I knew she had said those words for a reason. Probably more than one.

"Then, you can do whatever you want."

"Fuck," I murmured. "You might regret saying that."

"I guess we'll—"

I cut off her words when I lunged forward and sucked one side of her pussy lips into my mouth. "Mmm," I moaned around the taste of her and then did the same thing to the other side.

As I moved to lift my head to catch my breath, I caught her arm coming up, as if involuntarily, before going straight back down to the bed.

I kneaded the inside of her thighs and blew on her clit. "Rayne. Rayne, look at me."

She tilted her chin down.

"I know I said there wouldn't be any lessons, but I was wrong." I looked at her hand. "If you want to touch me or touch yourself, you do it. If I want you to do something, I will let you know, but I don't ever want you to hold back because you're afraid."

"What if I do the wrong thing?"

I shook my head. "You won't ever do the wrong thing. You might do something I don't like. Just like I might do something you don't like. But that's what communication is for. But as far as doing something wrong, I don't think you can."

The corner of her mouth tipped up in a smile.

"Now that we have that settled, I'm going to eat my pussy, and you're going to come." Shoving my mouth against her cunt, I drew her tight nub between my lips.

Her hips arched off the bed as the sound, "Oh...oh...oh," tumbled out of her.

Releasing the pressure, I swirled my tongue around her clit and licked my way down until I reached her taint. I was tempted to go further, but that would have to wait. This was our first night together, and some women were turned off by anal sex. It was best not to risk it right off the bat.

I made my way back up to her center, where I buried my face. I wanted to smell and taste her and lick the juices that coated her there. Letting myself enjoy her for a few minutes, I did just that. She tasted just as good as she had last night. Maybe even better. I could feast on her cunt all night, except I knew it wouldn't be enough to get her off. And my dick was starting to scream at me. The fucker had no patience.

Moving back up to her sweet spot, I sucked on her clit once more as I pushed two fingers inside her. Finding her G-spot, I went to work on making her soar.

I raised my head just enough to bark out, "Tell me

before you come." And as I did, I noticed her hands were on her breasts.

She had taken note of what I'd said.

That made me all the more determined to bring her to orgasm so that I could fuck her and make her come a second time all over my cock.

I worked her hard, but even as her breathing deepened and her pelvis started to rotate, I didn't change my rhythm. Too many men thought that women came the same way men did. As we got closer to orgasm, we often needed more speed and pressure, but women were different, and what they needed most was consistency.

So, when Rayne said, "Right there," I knew I needed to keep doing exactly what I had already been doing.

I didn't stop; I didn't go faster. I just kept my pace slow and steady.

And it wasn't long before I was rewarded with her crying out, "I'm going to come."

And as her core squeezed my fingers and flooded my hand with her orgasm, that was when I dragged her nub between my teeth and lightly bit down.

"Oh my God," Rayne yelled and grabbed on to my hair. She held my head down until she couldn't take it anymore and pushed me away.

Jumping to my feet, I threw myself over her and between her legs.

I shoved my cock inside her, not wanting her to come all the way down after her climax, but I hadn't anticipated how good she'd feel. I should have known because I had already felt how snug she was with my hand. Also, I hadn't had sex without a condom since sometime in high school, when I'd been young and reckless. The feel of Rayne's tight, wet, bare cunt was almost my undoing.

Almost.

But this wasn't my first fucking, and I wasn't about to bust a nut before I made her come again.

"You feel amazing," I made sure to tell her before I took her mouth, hesitantly at first in case she didn't want to taste herself.

But she immediately opened for me, and I plunged my tongue inside.

Her ass was still on the end of the bed, so I planted my feet on the floor and began to pump in and out of her.

With every thrust inside, she got wetter, soaking my cock. I knew there was no way I was going to last like I wanted to. In a battle of wills, my dick was going to win over my brain.

Remembering how Rayne had touched herself as I ate her cunt, I abandoned her mouth, and I went for her breasts. I tested each to see if she responded more to one than the other, but both seemed to turn her on. With a tug on each nipple, she gripped my dick with her pussy, as if there were a straight line from each tip to her core.

"Tell me when you're going to come again," I told her.

"I'm close," she said, clawing my back.

"Yeah"—I pinched one nipple—"I can tell." And I took the other between my lips.

Using my free hand, I slipped it between us to find her

clit. I pounded into her, hitting her G-spot with each thrust, and twisted her nipple with my finger as I bit down on the other.

"I'm going to come again. No. *Fuck*. I'm coming."

Yeah, you are.

She shattered in my arms, and her pussy drenched my cock, to the point that I could feel it dripping down my balls.

As soon as she was on the tail end of her orgasm, I grabbed on to her hips and yanked her toward me, wanting to be inside her as far as I could go. I nuzzled her cleavage with my nose, slammed into her two more times, and sank my teeth into the flesh of her breast as I poured myself deep inside her with a roar.

ELEVEN

RAYNE

SOMETHING WAS DRAGGING ME FROM EXCELLENT sleep, and I tried to fight it, but I lost.

The source of my discomfort was my annoying bladder.

As I rolled onto my back, I realized two things. The first was that I was naked. The second was that I was in Cade's bed.

It wasn't any wonder why I'd been sleeping so well. I'd had three orgasms last night after two rounds of sex. I needed to try that trick more often. Not necessarily the sex part, but I could do the orgasms myself.

I pushed back the covers and rose from the mattress, careful not to wake Cade. My vagina was a little sore, but that was because Cade was hung like a horse. I had never been with someone of his size before, and now, I knew why he was so confident all the time. His good looks got women to come home with him. His big dick and exceptional skills made them stay.

Until he kicked them out.

I almost snorted at my own joke and hurried to use the bathroom in the hall, bypassing the one in his bedroom so I wouldn't wake him up.

Flipping on the light, I made a beeline for the toilet. But once I was finished and went to wash my hands, I caught my reflection in the mirror, and I almost thought I was looking at a stranger. My hair was a mess—it needed a good brushing—my cheeks were flushed, and I had a red bite mark on the inside of my breast.

I brushed my fingertips over it, and my body did a little shudder. I was one of Pavlov's dogs, and my body remembered everything Cade had done to me in bed. It was surprising that not only had his bite not hurt me, but I had also loved it.

Dropping my hand, I rolled my eyes at myself. Of course he was good in bed.

"You already knew that. Quit acting so surprised," I whispered to myself.

I needed to remember to not let great sex cloud my brain or my feelings.

With a little bit of disgust at myself, I flicked the light switch off and headed back to his room.

His breathing was slow and even. Thankfully, I hadn't disturbed him, but as I looked at the clock, I wasn't sure what to do. Maybe I should have been louder, so he could throw me back on the bed and fuck me again, but he didn't move a muscle.

It was after two in the morning, and I knew how Cade felt about spending the night with women he slept with. He tried to avoid it as much as possible.

I was shocked he hadn't kicked me out earlier, and I didn't want him to get the wrong idea about me if he found me in his bed in the morning. I wanted more great sex, but I didn't want him to worry I was becoming attached to him. And after my reaction in the bathroom, I should leave before I worried myself.

I quickly swept my clothes up and carried them to the bathroom. After getting dressed, I did my best to finger-comb my hair, just in case I got pulled over or something. Then, I tiptoed down the stairs and snuck out the front door to head home.

The second time that morning, I was being pulled from sleep, except this time, it was by my phone ringing.

I was exhausted. After I had gotten home from Cade's, I had showered and crawled back into bed. It felt like I had slept for only twenty minutes. I didn't care who was calling me; I wasn't ready to get up.

I pulled my covers over my head and settled back in as my cell quieted. Slumber was just about to drag me back under when my phone rang again.

I almost ignored it once more, but the thought that it

might be an emergency crossed my mind. Reluctantly, I cracked open one eyelid to see it was still pitch-black outside.

The screen was too bright to read, so I aimed for the green circle and swiped it.

"What?" I answered in lieu of a hello.

"Where the fuck are you?"

Huh?

"Cade?"

"Who else would it be?" He sounded outraged, but I didn't understand what the big deal was.

"I don't know, dude. I'm trying to sleep."

"Dude?" I could hear him take a deep breath. "Where the fuck are you, Rayne?"

"In my bed, like a normal person is at"—I squinted at my alarm clock—"four twenty-two on a Sunday morning."

"That was a rhetorical question. You know what I meant."

No, I did not, but I didn't really care at the moment either.

"Look, I'll call you back later. Once I'm fully awake."

"Rayne—"

I hit End, turned my phone on silent, and went back to sleep.

"You are in so much trouble."

The deep voice right next to my ear had me on full

alert. For a moment, I had an absolute freak-out until I recognized Cade's smell and voice once I was fully awake. Thankfully, it was my friend who had my garage code and not some stranger who'd broken into my house in the early morning.

I rolled onto my back and scowled at him. "You *scared* me."

He got nose to nose with me. "You *left* my bed."

It was too dark to see his face, but I could tell he was mad.

"I don't understand," I said as I tried to sit up.

He pushed me back down. "I woke up, and you weren't there."

"That was kind of the whole point of leaving," I pointed out.

"Are you purposely being obtuse?" His voice was still firm, but I also caught a hint of humor in his tone, like he couldn't believe he was having this conversation.

"No."

"I'm seeing that now." He stood, turned on my bedside light, and lifted the sheet from my naked body. "Why did you leave, Rayne?" His tone was less heated and more even. Starting at my neck, he ran his fingertips down my body. "I woke up hard and aching for you." He paused at the bite mark.

I swallowed, trying not to let his touch affect me there. "I know how you feel about women spending the night, and vice versa. You don't like it." I shrugged. "So, I left."

His hand continued down, over my belly and in between my legs. He froze. "You showered?"

He said it as a question, but it sounded more like a statement. I wasn't sure if I should answer.

He gently pushed a finger into me, where I was already getting aroused again. "You washed my seed from you."

I opened my mouth, but I didn't really know what to say.

He pulled his hand from my body and brushed my desire over the teeth marks he'd left. "At least you still have this," he said in a low voice, as if he was thinking out loud rather than speaking to me.

I cleared my throat and sat up against my headboard. "I don't understand," I whispered. "Why did you want me to stay? Why do you want to...mark me?"

"What did I tell you yesterday at lunch?"

I licked my lips. "That you get me whenever and wherever you want. And that you need full access to me all the time."

"And?" He pulled his shirt over his head and kicked off his jeans. He wasn't wearing underwear, and his dick stood out from his body, long, thick, and proud. "And?" he asked again.

I met his eyes.

"You can have my cock in a minute. I need you to answer my question first."

"And..." My brain was firing blanks now.

Cade sighed, leaned over, putting our faces close, and pushed two fingers into me. "And this pussy is mine." He thrust his fingers in and out a few times. "Technically, I said, I need full access to *your pussy* all the time, but I like how you said it better."

I moaned and closed my eyes.

He stopped. "Rayne."

I lifted my lids.

"You'd best pay attention."

I nodded twice.

"I get full access to *you* at all times." His gaze roamed my face. "Your mouth, your breasts, your ass"—I gasped—"and your cunt." He rubbed his fingers over my G-spot, and my back arched with a cry. "This pussy is mine, Rayne. Mine." He slowly shook his head. "I don't care if it's only thirty days. You're mine." He got nose to nose with me again. "And that means you don't leave my bed until I say you do. Do you understand?"

"Yes." My voice sounded shaky, not because I was scared, but because I was incredibly turned on.

"Good girl."

I whimpered, and Cade looked down at his hand.

"You just soaked my hand." He tilted his head back up to me. "It's too bad you're in trouble."

"What—what are you going to do to me?"

"It's not so much what I'm going to do, but more like what you're not going to do."

What does that mean?

He knelt on the bed, in between my thighs.

"I'm going to fuck you. Definitely once. Most likely

twice. Possibly three times. And you're not going to come until I say you can."

My jaw dropped. "You can't be serious."

"Dead. Dead serious." He squeezed my clit with his thumb and index finger. "You left me, and you washed my cum from your body, so you don't get to come until I've filled you at least once." He lifted a shoulder. "Maybe twice."

"Joke's on you, Cade. I've had sex plenty of times without having an orgasm."

He tilted his head. "Did you not come on my cock earlier?"

"Yeah. So?" I wanted to seem unaffected, but I sounded like a bratty teenager instead.

He smirked and did something with his hand that had my hips flying off the bed.

"Hear that? That's the sound of your pussy gushing for me." He ripped his fingers from my body and lifted his palm to show me. "I'm not your ex or any other guy you've ever been with before. It's best you remember that."

He was so right about that.

Leaning back, he yanked me down until I was flat. He grabbed his thick length and placed it at my entrance. He nudged the head between my lips and met my eyes. "Remember, you don't come until I say you do."

"Okay," I agreed.

Maintaining eye contact, he slowly sank completely inside me, stretching me and filling me full.

"Fuck, you feel good."

So did he. There was no way I was going to last.

But in the end, I didn't have to. He let me come before he even did, and I soon realized my real punishment was too many orgasms. And it was only after I begged him to stop and promised to never leave him again that he relented.

Then, and only then, did he pull me in his arms and let me sleep. When I woke up later that afternoon, he was the one who had left me.

I had a feeling I was in deep trouble.

TWELVE
RAYNE

When I finally pulled myself from my bed on Sunday afternoon, Cade had sent me a text, telling me he had gone into work and that he hadn't wanted to wake me, so I hadn't been completely ditched.

It was kind of sweet, but I also wondered if he needed to take a step back from me because I didn't see him the rest of the day. He'd seemed so possessive of me, yet he'd made it clear in the beginning that we weren't going to fall in love with each other.

But I figured whatever issues Cade had, he needed to deal with them. I was going to enjoy sex with him, then hopefully find someone who wanted to be in a relationship.

I also hadn't heard back from him since I'd replied to his text about him going into work, so when my phone vibrated on my desk on Monday morning, I picked it up, wondering if it was him. I had no idea when we were getting together next, and while I didn't mind him calling the shots, it would be nice to know what was going on.

But it turned out to be my brother.

> Beau: What did you do the rest of the weekend?

Kind of an odd question. But before I could answer, he sent another text.

> Beau: I didn't hear from you after you left the restaurant, and then I drove by Cade's house on Saturday, and your car was there.

Oh shit.

Cade and I hadn't thought that through, especially since he lived close to my brother and Em.

Panicking, I quickly called Cade because I didn't know what to say, and I knew my brother could see I had already read his messages.

I just hoped Cade answered since he was probably at work. After three rings, I was beginning to think he wouldn't.

"Hey, Rayne," he greeted me. "What's up?"

He sounded normal. Maybe he wasn't worried about how things were between us.

A door closed in the background, and I figured he had gone into his office.

"Beau just texted me and mentioned my car was in your driveway on Saturday."

"What did you say?" Cade did not seem as worried as I was about what my brother had seen.

"Nothing yet. I don't know what to say."

"Tell him the truth."

"*What*? You want me to tell him we fucked?"

Cade groaned, but it came across as more of a *I'm in pain* kind of groan rather than a *you're frustrating me* groan.

"No. Tell him we went to lunch and you came to my work with me for a bit because it'd been a long time since you'd been here."

"You don't think he'll think it's suspicious?"

"He already does think that."

I bit my lip. "True."

"Besides, we're friends. I can hang out with you without Beau around."

We usually didn't, but he wasn't wrong.

"You're right. He'll only get more suspicious if I act suspicious."

"Text him back and let me know what he says. From now on, you can park in my garage when you spend the night."

A thrill went through me at him wanting me to spend the night.

I wasn't ignoring my brother's warning, but it did make me feel special that I was getting to see a side of Cade that no other woman did.

"Hold, please," I said.

Without hanging up, I quickly messaged my brother back.

> Me: Something came up on Friday, and I needed to regroup and be alone. It had nothing to do with you or Em. I still love you.

I smirked. Hopefully, adding that little tidbit would make him be less skeptical of my next text.

> Me: I hung out with Cade on Saturday. We went to lunch, and he took me to his work since I hadn't been to the restaurant in a long time. I'd forgotten how fancy it was.

> Beau: Weird.

> Me: Why? Cade and I are friends.

I cringed, crossing my fingers, hoping I hadn't come across as defensive.

> Beau: Just be careful. Cade isn't boyfriend material.

> Me: First, I'm an adult. Two, I've known Cade forever. I know how he is. Three, I just got out of a relationship. I'm not looking for a new one yet.

> Beau: Okay. I'm just checking.

Me: Thank you. But I'm fine.

I closed the app and put the phone back to my ear. "That's done," I told Cade.

"What did he say?"

"He warned me that you're not boyfriend material."

Cade snorted. "What did you say?"

"That it's fine because I'm only using you for your cock."

He groaned again. "Jesus, Rayne."

I chuckled. "I'm kidding. I told him I already know that about you and I'm not looking for a relationship after just getting out of one."

"Yeah, well, hearing you say things like 'we fucked' and you talking about my cock makes me wish you were using it right now." He grunted. "Now, I'm hard."

I grinned, loving that I, Rayne Thompson, had the power to make Cade Nichols hard. And it might be fun to see what else I could do.

"Yeah, well, hearing you say that makes me wet."

"*Goddammit.*"

I laughed out loud.

"You're in for it now." His words were threatening, but I could hear the smile in his voice.

"I mean...you do owe me some lessons. This weekend was great, but I need some pointers."

He snorted.

What did that mean?

Cade dropped his voice low. "Speaking of cock, do you like sucking it, Rayne?"

I sighed. "No," I reluctantly admitted. "But I wish I did."

And I really did. I wanted to be one of those women who got off on giving head.

"I don't hate it," I added so he fully understood where I was coming from. "But I definitely don't love it either."

There was too much silence on the other side of the phone.

"Cade? Did I mess up? *Shit*. Is this something I should lie about? Make it seem as if I like it more than I do?"

"*Fuck no.*"

Oh. I hadn't expected such a strong response.

"You should never do something you don't want to do sexually."

"Except when I'm with you, right?" I joked.

"Baby, you're going to *love* everything I do to you."

Dammit. Now, I really was wet.

"But keeping that in mind, if you ever want to stop, just say *Beau*."

"Beau?"

"Yeah. If you bring up your brother, I will immediately stop what we're doing."

"Kinky."

"No. Not kinky. That's the point." He made a gagging sound.

I bit my lip so I didn't laugh too hard.

"Okay, so I'm writing these two things down: Don't do

anything I don't want to do in bed. And Beau is our safe word."

"Liar. You're not writing them down."

"You're right; I'm not. But what if I told you I wanted you to teach me to give better head? And maybe even teach me how to love it?"

His breathing was heavy through the phone.

"I'll be there tonight after work. But first, I have to stop somewhere and pick something up."

"What's that?"

"You'll see when I get there."

I held my breath. "I can't wait."

"Fuck. Me neither."

"See you tonight."

"See you tonight."

I moved to end the call.

Until I heard, "Oh, and, Rayne?"

"Yeah?"

"Keep your garage open for me, and I want you naked when I get there."

And with that, he ended the call.

THIRTEEN
RAYNE

I WAVED AT MY NEW FRIENDS AS I HEADED FOR THE table at one of our favorite restaurants to meet for lunch.

Vivian Stern and Delaney St. James were my partners in the Women in Law program, started by the mayor, Nadine Evans.

While I worked as a prosecutor for the county, Vivian was a lawyer in the private sector, and Delaney was a family court judge. Nadine had wanted lawyers with a variety of jobs to let young women know that there was more than one option when going into the field.

As far as I knew, the three of us were only doing this for one school year, and next year, Nadine planned to recruit different lawyers, which made sense. The three of us were just the tip of the iceberg of what one could do with a law degree.

And while it took time out of my already-busy schedule, I really liked going to schools and talking to the kids. Plus, I'd made two new friends in the process.

The three of us weren't visiting a school today. We were simply getting together for lunch.

"Hey, ladies," I said as I took a seat next to Delaney in the booth. "Sorry I'm late."

"It's fine," Vivian said. "We already ordered your usual for you."

I grinned and picked up the water that was sitting in front of me to take a sip. "Thank you."

Vivian had messaged me and asked me what I wanted when I told her I was running behind.

"You look very happy this morning," Delaney said, leaning back and scanning me from head to toe.

"Do I?" I smiled coyly. "Maybe it's because I'm free of my ex."

The two of them had watched me be unhappy with my relationship for months. The last time I'd seen them, I had just broken up with Brett, so my emotions had still been a little raw. But today, I was more than glad we'd broken up.

"Nah." Delaney shook her head. "You met someone and had sex this weekend. You look like you've been thoroughly fucked. Something I never saw you as when you were dating your ex. No wonder you're so happy."

I laughed. "Delaney, do all judges talk like that?"

She shrugged and smiled. "I don't know because I only see them at work, and I certainly don't speak like this at work."

"Are you trying to avoid the question?" Vivian asked me.

I frowned. "What question? Delaney didn't ask me anything."

While technically true, I knew exactly what Vivian had meant. And when we'd first met, Vivian would have avoided all bedroom talk. But since she'd started dating her boyfriend, Dominick, she had loosened up a little.

Vivian rolled her eyes. "Tell me you're having lunch with a lawyer without telling me you're having lunch with a lawyer." She narrowed her eyes but couldn't stop the smile from crossing her face. "You know what I'm talking about."

"Yeah," Delaney said. "Did you have sex this weekend or not? Spill."

I looked at them both and was quite tempted to tell them all about Cade since they didn't know him or my brother, but I didn't. I would have to tell them about the bet and why my ex had broken up with me. I knew neither of these women would make me feel bad and would probably be outraged on my behalf, but it didn't lessen my embarrassment.

Especially when Vivian was in a new relationship with a very sexy man who made her incredibly happy—in and out of the bedroom. And while Delaney was single, I had recently met her ex-husband, who still looked at her like she was the most delicious meal he'd ever had when she wasn't looking. If he wanted her that much after they were divorced, I was sure the sex between them when they had been happy was out of this world.

"I hate to break it to you, ladies, but I did not meet anyone this weekend." It wasn't a lie. I shrugged. "I think I'm out of the post-breakup slump."

"Hmm." Delaney pursed her lips.

I laughed but really wanted to be done with the subject. "What's that?" I asked, nodding my head toward the envelope on the table.

"It's for Dominick. He's picking it up here rather than going to my office. The restaurant is closer to our apartment."

"Yeah, right," I said. "You just want to see him."

She lifted her chin, but her cheeks turned pink. "But I see him every night at home."

Delaney snorted just as the man we were talking about sauntered in.

Dominick Reyes was the total opposite of Vivian. She was reserved, never had a single hair out of place, and was dressed professionally. Her boyfriend was covered in tattoos, had an unruly hair and beard, and almost always wore jeans and a T-shirt. Yet, somehow, they fit together.

"Hey, baby," he said, sliding in next to Vivian and giving her a kiss on the mouth.

"Hey," she said, her eyes full of love as he turned to pick up the envelope.

"This for me?" he asked just as the server brought our food over.

"Yes."

As the waitress set our plates in front of us, Dominick turned toward Vivian.

He muttered, "Thanks, baby," and kissed her on the side of the neck.

A second later, Vivian squeaked as she jumped in her seat one second and almost melted the next.

"Anything else?" our server asked, barely glancing around at us, her mind most likely on what she had to do next.

We all said no, and she left.

"Yum," Dominick said. "Everything looks delicious." He pulled his hand out from under the table and stuck the tips of his fingers in his mouth. "Tastes delicious too."

"But you didn't try anything," I said before what he was actually talking about clicked in my brain. "Oh," I murmured, like the bonehead I was.

Dominick smirked. Vivian turned the darkest shade of red I'd ever seen anyone become. And Delaney snickered.

We all stared at each other for a few seconds before Dominick broke the silence.

"See you two at our St. Patrick's Day party." He kissed Vivian on the cheek, hopped to his feet, and adjusted his erection. "And I'll see you tonight, babe."

St. Patrick's Day was in less than two weeks. I'd almost forgotten Vivian and Dominick were having a party. I'd need to tell Cade I was busy that night.

"Don't forget that we have to go to Spencer's school this evening," Vivian reminded her boyfriend.

"Fucking kid is the worst cockblock," he mumbled

under his breath as he spun around and strode away.

As soon as Dominick was gone, Delaney said, "Damn, Vivian, you are one lucky girl," at the same time I said, "What did he do to you under this table?"

Vivian sighed and unwrapped her silverware. "You two aren't going to let this go, are you?"

"Nope," Delaney and I said together as we both dug into our food.

She rolled her eyes. "I can't believe I'm telling you this," she grumbled and looked at us. "Let's just say that there was a misunderstanding between Dominick and me, and I lied to him. So, my punishment is, I can't wear underwear for a month."

My eyes rounded as I remembered how Cade had had me go without underwear on Saturday. Was this something a lot of guys did? Had I been missing out all this time?

Vivian continued, "And he likes to check to make sure I'm following my penance. But really, he just uses it as an excuse to touch me."

Delaney's jaw was practically on the table. "I—I'm speechless. I have no words."

Vivian chuckled.

"Actually, I have so many questions; I don't know where to start." Delaney leaned forward, looking concerned. "I can't believe you go along with it. He doesn't really punish you, does he?"

Vivian's eyebrows rose. "You mean, are we into BDSM? Or do you mean, is he controlling? Either way, the answer is no. I'm going along with it because I did lie to him and because it makes him happy." She smiled. "Also because it's hot and I love it when he touches me." She shook her head in disbelief. "I have never been boy crazy in my life—not even as a teenager—but that man does something to me."

"I'm jealous," I admitted. "I've never had that kind of relationship." The closest I'd ever come to it was Cade, and that wasn't a relationship. "I really need to put myself out there more."

"Don't be too jealous," Vivian said. "It's not that warm outside yet."

"Dominick doesn't care that you're cold?" Delaney looked worried again.

"He would if I said something, but I have less than a week left. And I'm kind of going to miss it." She smiled, her eyes unfocused. "When I get home from work, he just bends me over and..." Straightening in her seat, she cleared her throat. "You get the idea."

"Yeah, that didn't make me less jealous at all," I said sarcastically.

Delaney gave me a sad look. "You'll find someone."

I thought about all the guys I'd dated. "I don't know about that."

"Vivian?" A man was walking by our table but stopped in his tracks when he noticed her.

"Hugh." She grinned, scooted out of the booth, and gave the guy a hug.

"This is the kind of guy I pictured Vivian with,"

Delaney whispered in my ear.

She wasn't wrong. The guy was in a suit, had his hair styled with a professional cut, and had a clean-shaven face.

Vivian stepped back. "Delaney, Rayne, this is my cousin, Hugh."

Ahh. It made sense now.

"Hugh, these are my friends."

Vivian's cousin reached over and shook Delaney's hand and then mine. He smiled at me.

"It's very nice to meet you," he said to the both of us.

"You too," I said as he pulled his hand away.

"We've never met any of Vivian's family before," Delaney said.

Hugh laughed. "This one is always busy." He pointed a thumb at Vivian, who rolled her eyes. He turned to her. "My mom told me you have a boyfriend and he moved in with you?"

Vivian nodded.

"She keeps the family in the dark too," he told Delaney.

"I'm a busy woman," Vivian protested.

"I get it. I am too." Hugh smiled. "Busy, that is. We should get together and catch up sometime."

Vivian smiled. "We should. We can double date."

Hugh shook his head. "I'm single now."

Vivian pursed her lips. "And you're giving me crap about not telling anyone anything. Jerk."

"I guess I deserve that." He squeezed his cousin's elbow. "Speaking of busy, I'm meeting someone for lunch, but I really would like to get together and meet this guy of yours."

"I'll call you," Vivian said.

Hugh said good-bye, and she slipped back into her seat.

"Did you hear that, Rayne? My cousin is single."

Delaney elbowed me. "Maybe the universe heard you." She looked at Vivian. "You should invite him to the party since Rayne is going to be there."

"Great idea. I might actually look forward to the event." Vivian, who'd needed to be convinced by Dominick to have the party in the first place, looked at me. "Hugh's an investment banker, and his ex-girlfriend used to brag about how good he was in bed."

My eyes followed the direction Hugh had gone, and I watched as he sat across the table from another man. Vivian's cousin was good-looking and seemed nice. He wasn't as sexy as Cade, but once my month with him was up, I would need to move on. Someone Vivian knew and trusted might not be a bad place to start.

"Do you think he'd even be interested in me?" I asked Vivian. I didn't want to put her on the spot, but as a thinner woman, she probably didn't always think about how guys felt about someone who looked like me. "Because if all his exes are skinny, I can already tell you, he's not going to be."

"Nope. Hugh's never dated a skinny woman in his life. According to him, he likes his girlfriends to have meat on their bones." Vivian smiled. "Think about it."

"I think I will."

FOURTEEN
CADE

I scowled down at Rayne. "You're not naked."

She laughed. "I just got home from work."

"That's probably a good thing because I need you to take everything off but your underwear."

She laughed, and it made me smile.

"What's so funny?"

"It reminded me of something at lunch today."

My eyebrows arched. "What in the world happened at lunch that made you think of getting naked?" An image of Rayne having lunch with some handsome lawyer guy had me frowning. I stepped closer and pulled her to me. "Or maybe the better question is, *Who were you having lunch with?*"

She placed her hands on my chest. "I had lunch with Vivian and Delaney. They're—"

"I know who they are," I said as I relaxed.

Rayne blinked up at me. "You do?"

I scratched my head. Maybe I didn't. "I thought they were part of your Women Doing Law thing."

"It's Women in Law, but, yes, that's who they are."

I grinned. "Then, I was right."

She shook her head as the corners of her mouth slowly turned up. "You...surprise me."

"How so?"

"I dated Brett for over a year, and you don't remember a single thing about him. I've been doing the Women in Law thing for a few months, and you haven't even met Delaney or Vivian, yet you remember." She chuckled. "Maybe I'm more baffled than surprised."

There was nothing to be baffled about. Brett was a pissant. I had remembered him, but I had told Rayne I didn't the other night because he wasn't good enough for her. I was glad they'd broken up, and it had nothing to do with our little agreement to help each other.

"Speaking of surprises, I have something for you."

Her eyes lit up. "You do?"

I picked up the small brown paper bag I had set down when I first came into her house and grabbed her hand. "Let's go to your bedroom, so I can show it to you."

"Is this why I have to get naked?" she asked as she followed behind me.

"Yep."

"So, it's a sex present?"

Grinning over my shoulder, I wiggled my eyebrows. "That's the best kind."

When we reached her room, I looked around.

"Where's your lube?" I figured her nightstand was the safest bet for where she stored it.

"I don't have any."

My eyes rounded. Didn't she ever pleasure herself? If not, that was something I was going to need to add to her lessons. "None?"

She shrugged. "I don't need any." Laughing, she said, "When I'm horny, I get plenty wet without any extra help."

Oh, trust me, I fucking noticed.

Which again brought up the question, *How could anyone claim she was bad in bed?* Wet pussies were the best, and hers seemed to get soaked.

But we'd only spent one night together. There were things I still didn't know. Like, until this morning, I hadn't known she didn't like blow jobs, and until this moment, I hadn't known she didn't have any lubrication in her house.

"So, everything off but my underwear?"

"Yeah." I opened the bag I'd brought with me and the box that was inside. I removed the gift from the adult store that I had stopped at on the way here before shoving it in my pocket.

When I turned back to Rayne, she was naked, except for a pair of purple panties.

"Dammit, woman, are you ever going to let me undress you? I turned around for two minutes..."

Laughing, she shrugged. "I'm efficient. Besides, you did tell me to be naked when you got here."

I lifted a finger. "Okay, I did say that. But once I saw you were still dressed, I imagined doing it myself."

She patted my arm like I was a little kid and said, "Next time."

I snorted. "Next time?" I stepped forward, using my body to crowd her backward toward her bed. "We'll see because, now, I'm picturing you naked on my bed when I come home tomorrow."

She sucked in a breath. "We're doing this again tomorrow?"

I brushed my thumb over her bottom lip when we reached the mattress. "We're doing this every night this week."

"But what if I have plans?"

I lifted a brow. "Do you?"

"No, but I could."

Cupping the back of her neck and pulling her mouth up to mine, I quickly kissed her hard. "Yes, you do. I just told you that you have plans with me every night."

She smiled. "I guess you did."

I smashed my lips down on hers again and swept my tongue into her mouth. Her arms immediately wrapped around my back as she moaned and rubbed herself against me.

Rayne was a great kisser, and I honestly could spend time just worshipping her mouth for hours, but we had a lesson to get to.

I lifted my head and watched her blink up at me.

"Lie back on the bed." My voice was huskier than it had been ten minutes ago.

"But I thought we were—I thought I was going to—"

I dropped my chin. "What did I tell you about listening to me?"

Rather than answer, she sat on the edge of the bed and lay down.

"Knees up."

As soon as her thighs were parted, I ran my knuckle over her underwear. They were damp, but not enough.

I leaned over her and kissed her again until I felt her body relax. Then, I kissed down her neck until I got to her chest, where I had somehow missed the red area on the inside of her breast.

I smiled. "My bite is still there."

When having a series of one-night stands, even if some of them were repeats, I always made sure to never leave any reminders of myself on women. I loved that I got to mark Rayne whenever, however I wanted. In fact, I liked that she thought of me when she saw the bite.

It was such a sudden turn-on that I was worried I was going to come if I so much as moved a centimeter.

I took a couple of deep breaths and brushed my lips over the mark. "Did I hurt you?"

"No. I mean, kind of. But I liked it."

I looked up to her face. "You are constantly surprising me."

She laughed. "How so?"

"I don't know. I guess I didn't think you'd be into pain, for one."

"I mean, if you bring out whips and chains, I'm going to say no. But if you want to tie me up and have your way with me, I'm game."

Closing my eyes, I dropped my head to her chest. "Rayne?"

"What?"

"No more talking, or we're never going to get to your lesson."

When she didn't respond, I lifted my head.

She rolled her lips inward to show me she would be quiet.

"You must really want that lesson," I whispered.

She nodded, and excitement filled her eyes.

Rayne was killing me. I was supposed to be turning her on, not the other way around.

Refocusing my thoughts, I sucked a nipple into my mouth, harder than I needed to. I didn't know if I was testing the pain thing with her or if I was punishing her for making me almost lose my head. But she moaned and dug her nails into my scalp.

After both her nipples were hard and swollen, I stood back to test her readiness. I slipped my forefinger under the crotch of her panties and skimmed her lips.

"Perfect," I told her and pulled her gift out of my pocket.

"What's that?" she asked.

I lifted it up to show her what I was holding. It was a

wearable G-spot and clitoral vibrator that almost matched her underwear in color.

"Ooh, what did I do to deserve that?"

Be fucking sexy as hell.

Rubbing the five-inch shaft through the wetness of her desire, I told her, "I'm going to put this inside you."

Once it was thoroughly coated, I gently pushed it between her lips until the only thing left was the base, which lay flat against her clit. The vibrator was snug inside her even though it was smaller than my shaft, reminding me of how tight she was. I had to stop myself from ripping it out and shoving my cock into her.

I forced myself to put her panties back in place and step back.

FIFTEEN
RAYNE

"On your knees, Rayne."

Cade held out his hand, and I let him help me up. I'd used a vibrator before, but always when lying on a bed. I'd never moved around with something inside me like this, and the sensation was definitely different. And it wasn't even on yet.

I slowly lowered to my knees.

Cade grabbed his phone, hit a few buttons, and looked down at me. "Unzip my pants and take my cock out."

Feeling nervous and excited, I followed his directions.

I pulled his shaft free of his jeans and boxers and stared. He was leaking pre-cum, and my pussy squeezed around the vibrator Cade had nestled there. I'd already known he was huge, but seeing it up close only made it seem larger. I didn't know if I was going to be able to do everything he wanted me to do. But I was willing to try, so I waited for my next set of directions.

"Do what you want."

My eyes flew up to his. "Huh?" My eyebrows shot together in confusion.

He smiled. "Just do what comes naturally. If I want you to stop or do something else, I will tell you." He caressed a hand over my head. "Remember, a part of this lesson is teaching you to love to give head. I don't want to make you do anything you don't want to do, and to help teach, I need a baseline. A place to start."

That made sense.

"But if you need a suggestion, start with the head."

"Can I use my hands?"

"You can use whatever you want as long as your mouth is involved."

Wrapping my fist around the base of his dick, I kissed the top and licked the fluid that had escaped his slit. I sat back and watched more leak out of him and smiled. Pushing to my knees again, I sucked just the tip of his cock in my mouth as he pushed something on his phone and made the vibrator start moving inside me.

I squeaked and jolted at the sensation.

"Careful with the teeth, Rayne," Cade instructed.

For not warning me he was going to turn it on, I gently scraped said teeth over his tip.

"*Fuck*," he barked out.

I sucked on the mushroom head and pulled it free of my mouth and laughed.

"I guess this means you're ready for the other part."

"What—"

He surprised me again with a press of his thumb. The front of the toy started vibrating over my clit.

I moaned.

"I take it, you like your gift?" He smirked.

I nodded.

"Suck me all the way into your mouth as far as you can."

Pulling him into my mouth with my tongue, I took him in as far back as possible. I was impressed with how much I could take, but it wasn't enough.

Cade cupped the back of my head. "It's okay, Rayne. You don't have to take all of me. I know I'm big. It feels good, no matter what."

I blinked up at him, his words reassuring me.

A thumb ran down my cheek. "You just need to have fun. Don't worry so much about what you're doing right or wrong. If your mouth is on a guy's dick, he's going to like it."

I released him. "But I want to make sure *you* like it."

He groaned and turned off the vibrator. "I do. Bring back a little bit of the feisty chick who just sassed me with her teeth." He bent down and kissed me on the lips. "Like I said, if I don't like something, I will tell you. But chances are, I will."

"But I like it when you tell me what to do."

Fire flared in his eyes, and I thought he was trying to hide how much he liked what I had just told him.

When he straightened, he had his domineering look in his eyes. "In that case, kiss my cock, lick it, and suck on it.

And when I'm ready to come, I want you to swallow. I don't care if you've never done it before. You're going to do it this time. You're going to do it for me."

I opened my mouth.

He held up a hand. "I don't want to hear if you've done that with other guys."

I rolled my lips inward to show him I was shutting up.

Turning on the toy again, he gripped the back of my head and tilted it up. "Does it feel good?"

"Yes," I whispered.

"Do you think you can come from it, or do you need something more?"

"Yes."

"Yes what?"

"Yes, I can come." I shifted my lower body and closed my eyes as I moaned.

"Open."

I lifted my lids and looked at him once more.

"I want you to come. I want you to come hard. But on one condition."

I licked my lips. "What?"

"You don't come until I do."

I sucked in a breath.

"You feel that orgasm coming for you, you do whatever you have to do to hold it off and get me there."

I released the air from my lungs.

"But once you taste my cum and it hits the back of your throat, you let yourself go." He raised an eyebrow. "Understood?"

"Yes, Cade," I said.

He kissed me on the top of my forehead. "Good girl." He nudged my head forward. "Now, take me in your mouth again and make me come."

I wasn't sure what else to do, so I continued with what had been working. Hearing him groan above me helped me with my confidence. I slid my fist down to the base of his cock and brought it up as I filled my mouth with as much length as I could.

His hand on my cheek brought my eyes up to him.

"I love the way your tongue feels against my cock."

His words caused my breath to hitch, but I tried to focus on getting him to fill my throat with his pleasure because I wasn't sure how much more I could take of this vibrator.

The hand on my cheek moved to reposition one of my hands to his tight balls. I fondled them and rolled them gently in my hand. Cade frowned and pulled his lip between his teeth, like he was trying to fight his urge to come.

"You are so good at this." He pushed something on his phone, and the vibrations kicked up a notch.

I could feel my orgasm building, and I was worried I was going to come before Cade. I didn't want to disappoint him.

Blocking out the sensations below my waist as best I could, I concentrated on him. In just a short time, I learned what he liked, so I stroked his root with my one fist while using the other to knead his balls. Then, I wrapped my lips around the rest of his cock and sucked over and over, milking him with my mouth.

Soon, his breathing grew more ragged as his dick jerked in my mouth every few seconds.

"Fuck, Rayne, don't stop."

"Hmm," I hummed around him to let him know I wasn't going to, and that seemed to be what set him off.

A thunderous shout bellowed from the back of his throat as his cock pulsed and his seed hit the back of mine.

As soon as I got my first taste, I exploded around the vibrator inside me. Not wanting to fall, I released him from my hands to hold on to his hips.

I kept Cade's shaft in my mouth until his orgasm was done before ripping my mouth away and panting as I dug my nails into his skin.

Cade caressed my head and neck until my body began to relax.

When I realized I might be hurting him, I quickly pulled my hands away. "Shit. I'm sorry."

He smiled and knelt down. "Don't ever be sorry for showing me just how good your orgasm is."

He reached into my underwear, finding the vibrator not where he'd put it.

"Fuck, Rayne, did you come so hard that you pushed it out of your body?"

I hadn't noticed right away. "I must have."

He held up the purple toy. "I've never been jealous of a vibrator before."

I chuckled. "That was pretty intense."

He brushed his lips over mine. "Good." He smiled. "My pleasure is your pleasure, Rayne. We're going to do this every night this week."

My eyes widened. "You mean, I'm going to give you a blow job while using the vibrator?"

"Yes. And once you associate my orgasm with yours, you're going to love giving head."

I thought I was already well on my way to doing that.

SIXTEEN
CADE

"Explain something to me." I rolled onto my side and rubbed Rayne's nipple between my finger and thumb.

She was lying on her back, eyes closed, looking content from the fucking I'd given her. "What's that?"

Abandoning her breast, I ran my hand down her stomach and between her legs. I liked feeling my cum in her. I grunted and rolled away. If I kept touching her, I'd never get my question out, much less get an answer.

"The night of the bet. When you offered your idea up to me and I told you no, you immediately thought it was because of your body. You're always so confident, but in that moment, you were the opposite." I picked up her hand. "I felt awful, you know. It'd never even occurred to me that you would think I said no because of your weight."

"You must not remember high school."

I chuckled. "I remember it very well."

"I meant, for me. You must not remember very well

how high school was for me. Or at least, what I went through."

She tugged her hand out of my grasp, and I felt her withdrawing.

Wanting her to know she had my full attention, I found the covers at the end of the bed, pulled them over us, and faced her again.

"I can sense whatever you're thinking about isn't good, but I want you to know, I had to cover you up because I can't resist you."

She smiled almost sadly and rolled toward me.

"In middle school, there was a small group of popular kids that called me Rayne the Train or Rayne the Plane." She winced. "Whatever they felt was bigger that day."

I wanted to find those kids and punch them in their fucking faces.

"In high school, the boys either ignored me or friend-zoned me. I often felt like I was invisible or a nobody. I don't know what's worse—to be made fun of or to be entirely undesired. Nobody liked me. Romantically. Sexually. I had friends, but I didn't have my first real boyfriend until college."

"I had no idea."

"And you wouldn't have. You and Beau were two years older than me. You were only in middle school with me one year and high school for two. And freshmen and sophomores were on opposite ends of the school from the juniors and seniors."

"What about Em?"

Em was only a year older than Rayne in school.

She shook her head. "Em didn't go to our middle school, and by high school, no one really cared about who was popular or not. I always feel like middle school is more like how they portray high school in movies."

"I can see that. There were definitely more popular kids in high school, but you're right. It seemed less important."

"It could have been worse. I was called mean names occasionally. I still remember some of those same kids stealing this other girl's backpack and throwing everything inside in the garbage."

"That's awful."

She gave me the side-eye. "You ever do anything like that?"

I scoffed. "*No.*"

To be honest, I had been too busy playing football and hockey, but I hoped even if I hadn't been, I wouldn't have been such an asshole.

"I'm glad. Anyway, it wasn't until I went to college that things changed. I met people who hadn't known me, growing up, but there were two things that definitely helped me become more confident."

A true smile was on her face now.

"There was this badass chick who lived in my dorm. She wore cool clothes when we went out. She would dye her hair all these fun colors. She didn't care what anyone else thought about her. And she had plenty of guys panting after her. The best part? She was fat. Like me. Until then, I

had never seen anyone who looked like me but acted like…
a thin person." She laughed. "It sounds funny to say, but I
don't know how else to say it."

I smiled at how animated she was.

"It was then that I learned different people liked
different body types. And it was also where I learned that
confidence really was attractive. Sure, I had read about it in
magazines, but it wasn't until I met her that I realized how
true it was."

"She sounds amazing."

"She was. Is. I think she lives in Arizona now, but she's
still big and beautiful."

"So, what was the other thing that changed you?"

Her lips slowly curled up, and she got an almost-
dreamy look on her face.

I had a feeling I wasn't going to like this part.

"I met my first boyfriend."

I was right. I didn't want to hear this. I was happy for
her, but I got a weird pinch in my chest at the mention of a
boyfriend.

"We had a class together. I thought he was cute, and he
actively pursued me. No one had ever done that before. He
was so good-looking; I worried he had asked me out on
some kind of bet his friends had made."

"But he didn't?" Was I a horrible person to almost wish
the guy had asked her out because of a bet?

Yes. Yes, I was, especially since she was here with me
now and not with him.

Rayne started laughing, as if she suddenly remembered

something. It took her several seconds before she could talk.

"We got together to study one night. I went to his dorm room, and he must have stepped out to go to the bathroom because the door was ajar. But he had left his computer open." She lifted her hand and gestured, as if she could actually show me what she had seen. "Right there, on his desk, staring me in the face, was the porn he'd been watching. The woman in the video was bigger than me, and that was when I realized he might really like me."

"What happened when he came back?"

"I heard him in the hall because the volume was down low, so I shut the top of his laptop. When he walked in, the blood drained from his face, and his eyes ping-ponged around the room as he looked at his computer and back at me. It had occurred to me that he might have left it like that on purpose, but there was no way he could fake his physical reaction. He looked like he was going to crap his pants, and I had to act like I had no idea what was going on. To this day, he doesn't know I saw that."

My eyes widened. "You never told him?"

"Nah. We dated for a year. I was only nineteen when we broke up. If I were dating him nowadays, I would tell him, but I was embarrassed about that stuff back then."

I wrapped my arm around her and pulled her close. "So, you learned that you were beautiful too."

"Yeah, I did. And once you told me you personally found me attractive, I saw no need to hide from you." She lifted a shoulder. "It's just that I know not everyone is going to be attracted to my body type. That happens a lot more than for thin body types, so I sometimes guard myself."

"I'm glad you don't have to do that with me."

"Me too."

Even though the thought of Rayne with her college boyfriend weirdly bothered me, I was glad she'd learned to see the beauty in herself.

A sudden thought occurred to me, and I leaned back. "He wasn't one of the assholes who said you were bad in bed, was he?" I didn't like to think of her with him, but if he ruined this wonderful story, I was going to be pissed.

She laughed. "No, even though I'm sure I was." She snorted. "But so was he. We were freshmen. He tried to please me, but he didn't know what a clit was. Or he did, but he had no clue how to find it."

"I know what a clit is," I stated rather smugly.

"I noticed." She kissed my chin and lowered her voice. "I also learned that you can find out a lot about people by the porn they watch."

Was this a hint that she wanted me to tell her what I enjoyed?

"What kind of porn do you watch?" Her first.

"I'm kind of boring. I like it when a guy is really into a woman, and I like it when a woman is really enjoying herself. A friend once told me I was putting myself in their place. That explains why I roll my eyes when I hear fake moans and noises. Why do men not care if the woman isn't into it?"

I shrugged. "I don't know. I'm not one of those guys."

"So, what kind of porn do you like?"

"I'm not picky."

She playfully pushed on my shoulder. "Cop-out. I told you. You have to tell me."

"I like a lot of stuff. And sometimes, it just depends on the day."

"I get that. But you have to have some favorites."

I grinned. "Creampies." And squirting, but I kept that one to myself. I didn't want Rayne to feel bad that she didn't do that.

Her eyes rounded. "Is that why..." She blinked and frowned. "Do you fuck everyone without a condom?"

"Nope. Just you. And one girl in high school, but that was me being young and irresponsible. Besides you, I always use condoms."

A smile slowly expanded across her face even though she tried to hide it. "That explains a lot."

"Like what?"

"The no-condom thing. I thought it was because of the way it felt, but now, I'm thinking it's also because you like to come in me."

I grinned. "Guilty." I loved seeing my cum in her.

SEVENTEEN
RAYNE

I TAPPED MY PEN AGAINST MY L-SHAPED DESK AS I lifted the phone receiver to my mouth.

"No, the revised report needs to be sent to me by the end of the day. That should be at the top of your priority list," I said to the associate attorney on the other end. "I need you to also put in a reminder call to the defense attorney's office for the missing files. They've been ignoring my emails. Let me know if they give you the runaround."

"I'll get right on that, Ms. Thompson. And I will let you know how the phone call goes."

"Thank you." I hung up the phone and quickly jotted down a few notes.

The sound of a throat clearing had me swinging my chair around to face my door.

"*Cade.*" I bolted out of my seat.

My brain immediately recalled the words he'd said to me over our discussion at lunch a little over a week ago.

"If I'm going to agree to this, I need full access to your pussy at all times."

So far, that had been in the evenings and on weekends. Sometimes in the morning before we both had to leave for work.

He'd also told me I should wear skirts to work, and today, I was in a dress.

"Damn, that was hot. I like the bossy side of you."

I smirked. *Just not in bed.*

"What are you doing here?" I asked calmly despite the pounding of my heart.

"I had to run an errand for work, and I was in the neighborhood."

All the stiffness left my body. He'd dropped in to say hi.

The corner of his mouth slowly rose in a smirk. "I'm also hungry." He strutted backward and closed my office door.

My mouth went dry. "What does that mean?"

He didn't really mean sex, did he? I was at work. I didn't have a lock on my door, so anyone could walk in.

"It means, you've been such a good girl this past week, sucking my cock every night. I almost think you're starting to like it."

I licked my lips. "Not almost. Not starting to. I do like it."

More like love it. The sounds that Cade made when I wrapped my mouth around him and sucked him to the back of my throat made me feel powerful. And the way he looked at me...it made me feel like I was the most gorgeous woman in the world.

We'd been experimenting with different positions too. I'd knelt on the floor, I'd lain between his legs, I'd lain on the bed while he stood, and one night, we'd sixty-nined. But I thought my favorite was when he had stood next to the bed while I was on my back with my head hanging off the mattress and I let him wrap a hand around my throat and basically fuck my face. Funny how that was the one where I'd had the least control and Cade had the majority, but it was the one I'd enjoyed the most.

I felt my core pulse, just thinking about it.

He stalked toward me. "Are you thinking about it right now?"

"That I like it when you come in my mouth?"

Cum was never going to taste the best, but there was something about his that I didn't mind.

Maybe it was the way he kissed me after, like he couldn't get enough of me.

I was really going to miss our bedroom fun when it was over.

Cade groaned and adjusted his pants. "Rayne, babe, you are making me hard."

In the last few days, he'd dropped the *babe* thing more than once. I didn't know if he even realized he said it.

Removing his hand, he held it up along with the other, as if he was surrendering. "Nope. No. I came here for you." He lowered his gaze to my crotch. "And for me. We've spent way too much time on you going down on me and not enough of me going down on you. I miss your taste."

My eyes widened in shock. "You like the way I taste?"

He cupped my face. "You are the most interesting mix of naughty and naive."

I frowned at him. "I wouldn't say I'm naive."

He pursed his lips, holding back a smile. "You're right. You're not. How about...you're a mix of experienced and inexperienced?"

"That's better."

He laughed and took my mouth. His lips were hard, and his tongue was soft. I sucked on it like it was his shaft, and before I could figure out what was happening, he pulled away.

"Take off your panties and go sit in your chair."

After sleeping together for over a week, I no longer hesitated when he gave me a command. Even though a part of me was nervous that someone might come in, the part that wanted him to eat me out was louder, so I might as well listen to her.

I slipped off my underwear and shoved them in the bottom desk drawer, where I kept my purse, then sat.

Cade eyed my armrests. "Do those move out of the way?"

"Oh. Yes, they flip up." I quickly snapped both of them upright.

"Perfect." He tapped a finger on his bottom lip, then crossed his arms and widened his stance. "Spread your legs and slowly lift the bottom of your dress and show me your pussy."

Sliding my bottom forward on the leather seat, I leaned back so my hips were forward and bared myself to him.

"So wet. I can see your cunt glistening in the light. I could stare at you all day."

Voices sounded in the hall, and he grimaced.

"Unfortunately, we don't have all day."

He dropped to his knees, and I watched in shock when he crawled underneath my big wooden desk.

He winked up at me. "This way, no one can see me if they walk in." My old desk had a finished back that went all the way to the floor. "I want you to enjoy this and not worry about getting caught."

I was about to tell him how sweet he was, but he yanked my chair forward and shoved his face between my thighs.

"Sorry, babe, we'd better make this quick."

He licked the seam of my lips, pulling each one into his mouth. It didn't do much for me physically, but mentally, I loved that he enjoyed that part of me. He continued north until he reached my clit and sucked. He used the flat of his tongue to flick and stroke the swollen nub, and my desire leaked onto my chair.

He groaned, moved his mouth lower, and slurped up my juices.

No man that I had been with liked giving me head as much as Cade. And that alone turned me on so much that when he reached my clit again, it only took one little nip from his teeth for me to come.

Latching on to his hair, I held him close and rode out my orgasm, rotating my pussy across his face.

When I was thoroughly satisfied, I dropped back in my chair and relaxed my fingers.

Cade scowled up at me. "I wasn't finished."

I smiled and shrugged. "Sorry, honey, maybe next time, don't do such a good job."

He chuckled and pushed my chair back so he could get out. "I didn't even need to hide," he said as he stood. Leaning over, he kissed me, making sure I got a taste of myself. "But I like you calling me honey. Keep doing that."

Smoothing my dress down, until I was alone and could put my panties back on, I said, "I'll think about it."

He lifted my chin. "It wasn't a suggestion."

"Noted, honey," I practically whispered.

He groaned and kissed me. "I'll see you later. It's going to be a long evening."

Before I could ask what he meant by that and whose place we were going to tonight, he was gone.

I sighed and let myself relax in my post-orgasmic bliss for a minute before I got dressed and went back to work. It was going to be a long afternoon.

EIGHTEEN
CADE

I drummed my fingers on the back of Rayne and Beau's parents' couch. Dinner was supposed to be ready soon, and everyone but Rayne was here.

> Me: Where are you? Is everything okay?

> Rayne: I just stopped to get gas after work.

Good. She was on her way.

> Rayne: Are you coming over tonight, or am I going to your place?

Oh shit. That wasn't a good sign.

"Hey, Beau?"

My best friend looked away from his wife, who sat in the recliner across from us, to me. "Yeah?"

"Where's your sister? Shouldn't she be here by now?"

Beau frowned at me, and I was sure he was wondering why I'd asked about Rayne, but at the moment, I didn't care.

Em gasped, her eyes huge. "Your mom didn't forget again, did she?"

Beau cursed under his breath. "Mom? *Mom!*"

Miriam Thompson poked her head around the corner from the dining room.

"Did you forget to tell Rayne about family dinner again?"

Miriam's face drained of color. "Oh no." She ran toward the kitchen. "Oh no, oh no. *Oh no, oh no, oh no, oh no.*"

"Rayne is going to be so hurt," Em said, looking like she was in pain herself.

I clenched my jaw. I knew Miriam loved Rayne, and the woman was like a second mother to me, but all I could think about was how, in high school, Rayne had felt invisible. Like a nobody. And now, her own mother had forgotten to invite her. I found myself angry with Miriam.

Beau pushed himself off the couch. "I'll be right back."

"What are you going to do?" Em asked to his retreating back.

"I'm going to tell my mom to not tell Rayne she forgot. Again."

"Maybe I should go," I said.

Em wrinkled her nose. "Why?"

"Because it's going to look really bad that Rayne wasn't invited, but I was."

She winced. "Oof. Yeah, I see where you're coming from, but Beau always comes up with something."

"Jesus, how many times has this happened?"

"Too many."

"Why was I never told about this?"

Em tilted her head. "Why would anyone have told you?"

Right. Because Rayne wasn't my girlfriend or anything.

I shrugged. "I guess I thought I knew everything that went on at the Thompson house," I mumbled.

It wasn't a great reason, but Em seemed to accept it.

I glanced down at my phone and realized I had missed a text.

> Rayne: You still there? LOL. Where are we going tonight?

Fuck. I didn't know how to respond.

Beau came barreling out of the kitchen. "Okay, so Mom is calling Rayne and asking her to come to dinner. She's going to tell her that they were going to have friends over, but the friends had to cancel. She has extra food, so she invited all of us to eat."

I unlocked my phone.

> Me: My place. Work for you?

I held my breath while I waited for her to respond.

> Rayne: Yes, but it might be later. My mom just called and invited me to dinner at the last minute. Is it okay if I come after?

I sighed with relief.

"Hey, asshole. Who the fuck are you texting over there?"

Without looking up, I flipped him the bird.

> Me: Oh, hey. I just got invited too. See you there.

Thankfully, my house was closer to her parents' than her work was. Same with Beau and Em.

I looked up at my best friend and gave him a cocky smile. "I'm texting your sister."

"Ha-ha. Very funny. Who you really textin'?"

Your sister. "None of your business."

Em grinned. "I bet it's the woman he's been forced to sleep with since you made the bet with him."

Beau smiled cunningly. "Oh yeah. Are you ready to call it quits yet?"

"Not even close," I said with satisfaction. Because I didn't have to force myself to do anything when it came to Rayne. "I'm going to win, so you'd better get ready to put in your notice at work."

Beau opened his mouth, but before he could say anything, Arthur Thompson walked into the living room. "Rayne will be here in ten minutes. Remember, everyone was invited at the last minute."

His son rolled his eyes at him. "Yeah, we know. It was my idea."

"Don't get mouthy with me. I'm not the one who forgot."

"Because you never invite anyone," Beau pointed out.

Arthur shrugged. "I don't get in trouble either." He spun around on his heel and left.

"If you ever turn into your dad, I'm divorcing you," Em told Beau.

"And I'll donate to her lawyer fund," I said.

RAYNE

"Oh, hey," I said, stopping when I saw Beau, Em, and Cade sitting in the living room. "You three look like you've been here awhile."

Em and Beau exchanged looks, but before I could ask what was happening, my mom rushed into the room and pulled me into her arms.

"I'm so glad you're here."

Since my arms were trapped under hers, I awkwardly patted my mother on the back. I looked at my brother over her shoulder, but he just shrugged.

"Thanks, Mom. You know it hasn't been that long since I saw you."

She stepped back and squeezed my biceps. "I know, but I just love you so much. You know that, right?"

"Are you sick or something?"

She laughed. "No."

"Is Dad?"

"No. Can't a mother just be happy to see her daughter?"

"Sure."

"Good." She released me and turned around. "Why don't you all go sit at the table? Your dad is already in there. The food will be ready in just a few."

"I'll help," I told her.

"No, you've been at work all day. Your brother can help me."

Beau sat up straight. "I can?"

Cade pushed his best friend in the knee with his foot. "Yeah, you can. Show your wife that you're not your father."

Em snorted.

It seemed like I had missed something.

But at least I wasn't alone.

"What does that mean?" Mom asked.

"Never mind." Beau stood. "Let's go get dinner on the table."

NINETEEN
RAYNE

My parents sat at the head and foot of the dining room table with Beau and Em on one side and Cade and me on the other.

It felt like a normal dinner, except I had to hold myself back from touching Cade. I was so used to doing that whenever I wanted—unless he told me not to. But then that meant he was the one touching me.

A couple of times, I stole glances at him to see if he felt the same way. So far, I couldn't tell. But he hadn't snuck any looks my way or tried to touch me under the table, like I had kind of hoped he would.

But then again, I didn't touch him either.

At the end of dinner, we took our dirty dishes to the kitchen, where Mom shooed us away, and my dad went to the den to watch television. It left the four of us sitting at the dining room table.

Beau sat back in his seat and put his arm around Em.

"Since we were interrupted earlier, how are you doing with the bet?" He narrowed his eyes. "For real this time."

I perked up at this. "When did you talk about it before?" I wanted to know everything Cade had to say.

"Right before you got here," Em supplied. "But Cade didn't give us any details since your mom walked into the room."

"Oh," I said, disappointed.

"And, yeah, Cade, we haven't seen you in over a week." Em looked at him with fake concern. "How are you holding up?"

Cade laughed mockingly. "I'm holding up just fine, thank you very much."

"Your dick isn't going to fall off from underuse?" my brother joked and glanced at me in the way people did when they thought the other person was going to get their joke.

I was laughing, but I realized that I needed to say something, or Beau and Em were going to think it was odd.

"I'm sure Cade and his hand are becoming well acquainted this month," I said.

"Fuck you," he said to my brother. "Fuck you," to Em and, "Fuck you," he said to me, this time with a look in his eyes that said he really was going to fuck me when we were alone.

I raised my eyebrows and scrunched up my nose. "Nah."

Beau and Em laughed as a hot palm landed on my thigh.

"Hard pass," I added because I was having fun, teasing him.

He squeezed my thigh. "I'll show you something hard," he growled.

My mouth dropped open, and my eyes bugged out, but I still couldn't help but laugh, knowing I'd gotten to him.

"*Cade*," my brother snapped.

Cade swung his head toward my brother. "*What?*" he snapped back.

"You can't have sex with my sister." Beau threw up his hands. "I mean, you already had sex with my wife."

I froze, and all thoughts of humor vanished from me. "What?" I practically whispered.

An empty feeling opened up in my stomach despite the home-cooked meal I'd just had.

When had this happened? How? Why was I just now finding out about this? And why did it make me feel sad?

"How are you okay with that?" I asked Beau as Cade squeezed my leg again.

I wanted to throw his hand off, but I couldn't. Not only would everyone know he was touching me, but then he would also know I was upset. And I'd promised not to develop feelings for him.

My brother shrugged. "It was back in high school. Before Em and I started dating." He put his arm around his wife. "We both liked her, but Cade hit on her first." He smiled at Em. "But I was the one who won her in the end."

Cade rolled his eyes, and I let go of the breath I'd been holding.

Even though I was still bothered by this new information, it had happened over a decade ago, and that made me feel better.

I didn't want to think about why it made me feel better though.

Em kissed her husband and looked at me. "Don't worry, Rayne. You're right about hard pass. It wasn't any good."

Cade scowled. "It was your first time. Of course it wasn't any good."

"Whatever you say. My second time was with Beau, and it was *much* better."

The feeling was starting to come back. Cade had taken Em's virginity? And the only other guy she'd ever slept with was Beau?

"Yeah, well, I don't really remember you being the best either," Cade said, clearly bothered by Em's assessment of him.

She cocked her head. "You came, didn't you?"

Cade snorted. "I was sixteen. A stiff breeze could have made me come."

Beau, laughing at the banter between his wife and best friend, looked at me and tilted his head. "Rayne, are you okay?"

No. Not at all.

Em was thin and had the perfect figure. No wonder Cade and my brother had liked her. Meanwhile, I couldn't even get one date back then. Not even from a manwhore like Cade.

And knowing he was Em's first ate at me. Did Cade hold a special place in her heart? Did she in his?

But I couldn't say all that, could I?

"I just can't believe no one ever said anything. How did I not know this?"

Em's smile fell. "Oh, Rayne, I'm sorry. We never meant to leave you out. I was a freshman. You were still in middle school. It was before the four of us began hanging out so much."

It made sense, and if that were the only thing bothering me, I wouldn't be so upset. Which meant I had to fake being okay.

So, I did the only thing I could think of. I made a joke.

"I suppose that speaks to how bad it really was. Em didn't want to relive the horror by thinking about it again."

My brother howled with laughter, and Em covered her mouth to semi-hide how hard she was cracking up.

Cade's eyes were narrowed, and his mouth was hard as his fingers dug into my skin, and I felt a little bad.

I was about to apologize when he talked first.

"I'll have you know, the woman I am seeing for the month loves my dick and is always satisfied."

He spoke to all three of us, but I knew his words were meant for me.

"Maybe she's faking it," Em offered.

"Nah. You can't fake a soaked pussy." He smirked. "Or the way it milks my cock when she comes." He looked at me and smiled. "Right, Rayne?"

My brother frowned in my direction. " 'Right, Rayne?' "

Our mom walked into the dining room before Beau could read too much into Cade's words.

"I forgot dessert. Is anyone in the mood for some?"

Beau finally took his eyes off me. "What did you make?"

"Nothing." Mom smiled. "But I bought your favorite pie from the store."

I frowned at her words. Why would she have bought Beau's favorite pie for dinner with my parents' friends?

"I'll just go get it," she said, spun around, and went back to the kitchen.

Everyone looked at me, like they were waiting for something.

"She forgot to invite me again, didn't she?"

Cade's parting words to me earlier that afternoon now made sense.

Beau shook his head, but Em looked like a statue.

"Yes," Cade admitted in a low voice.

"Thanks for telling me the truth," I told him.

Shaking off his hand, I turned in my chair and stood. "Don't tell Mom I figured it out."

"Don't go," Em said.

"I think it's best." I already felt like shit from what I'd found out about Cade and Em. My mom forgetting about me was icing on the fucking cake.

I didn't bother to message Cade that I wasn't coming over. I just went home and curled up in my bed to cry.

TWENTY

RAYNE

When my alarm went off in the morning, I wanted to pull the covers over my head and go back to sleep. Even though I had been out like a light all night, I felt like I hadn't slept a wink, and my body and mind were sluggish.

I was emotionally exhausted.

Last night, after I'd left my parents, my mom had tried to call me a couple of times, but I hadn't answered. I didn't want to hear her excuses for why she had forgotten to invite me to dinner for the five hundredth time if someone had let it spill that I had found out. And if she didn't know, I didn't want to pretend to be okay or lie about why I had left early.

I only wanted to be alone.

It had been too early for bed, but as soon as I walked in the door, that was what I did. I had put on some comedy show, hoping it would help me feel better. Not only about my mom, but also about what I'd found out about Cade and Em.

In the cold light of day, it didn't seem as big of a deal as it had last night. I was still bothered, but not as much.

I was more worried about why I was so bothered.

Was I developing feelings for Cade? I didn't think so. So, maybe it was because I felt like I was his second choice. I hardly felt like anyone's choice, and when I was, I was third, fourth, or fifth. I just wanted to be someone's first choice for once.

Okay, that wasn't fair to every guy I'd ever dated because they had chosen me. But breaking up meant that, in the end, I hadn't been the right choice.

I groaned.

I needed to stop feeling sorry for myself and focus on the reality instead of ruminating on the past.

There were guys who found me attractive, and I had a killer teacher in bed. Once this month was up, I was going to put myself out there. I was going to find someone, and I was going to keep him.

Unless I didn't want him anymore.

I laughed.

That's right, Rayne. You're going to break up with him *next time.*

An arm snaked around my waist. "What's so funny, babe?"

I jumped out of bed, my heart hammering in my chest.

"Cade, what are you doing here?"

He had been behind me, and I hadn't noticed he was there.

He opened one eye and squinted. "What do you mean? You didn't come to my house last night, so I came here."

"But...we didn't have sex." I still had my pajamas on, and I was dry between my legs.

"You were passed out when I got here, so I shut off the TV. I didn't want to wake you, so I came to bed later." He grinned. "Not going to lie though. Once I slipped into bed next to you, I was hoping you would wake up, so we could continue from where we'd left off at your work. But I knew, after dinner, you probably wouldn't be up for it anyway."

I stepped closer and sat on the bed, shaking my head in amazement.

He had come over despite knowing I might not be in the mood. And when he had gotten here and found me asleep, he hadn't left.

My heart started picking up speed for a different reason.

I frowned at my thoughts.

What had I just told myself about not having feelings?

Still, it felt good to know he'd wanted to be with me.

Cade opened his other eye and squinted harder. "I can't tell if you're upset or happy."

I laughed. He had probably seen a whole range of emotions cross my face.

"I'm...okay," I told him.

He grabbed my hand. "I'm sorry about your mom." He winced. "And I'm sorry I lied about just getting invited."

I gasped. "You lied about that? I thought only Beau and Em had been invited beforehand."

"Rayne..."

He moved to sit up, and I pushed his chest back down.

"I'm joking. I walked in, and all three of you were sitting in the living room. Obviously, you had been invited before last night."

Cade's eyebrows slammed together. "You're not funny. I was so pissed at your mom for forgetting to invite you. After everything you went through in high school, I don't care if she's like my second mother; I wanted to shake her for being so uncaring."

"You were mad at my mom because of me?" I asked in wonder.

"*Yes*. It was rude. And your dad wasn't much help."

I rolled my eyes. "He's usually not, and I should be mad at him, too, but he's not worth the energy."

"It's still shitty."

"Yeah."

"Are you going to say something to your mom?"

I shrugged. "What's the point?"

Cade jacked upright, wrapped his hand around the back of my neck, and put his nose to mine. "Because you shouldn't put up with anyone treating you like that, especially someone who claims to love you."

I appreciated what he was saying. I really did. It put warm fuzzies in my stomach. But when he had sat up, the

135

bedsheet had fallen down, and it was obvious that Cade was naked.

And I couldn't stop myself from looking at his beautiful body.

The thin piece of cloth slowly rose in his lap.

"Rayne," he snapped.

I pulled my eyes from his erection and licked my lips. "What?"

He nipped my bottom lip, and the corner of his mouth tipped up. "We're talking about something serious here."

"I know."

"Are you going to talk to your mom?"

"I don't know."

Cade pulled his hand from my neck and covered his crotch. "No cock until you talk to her."

My jaw dropped. "You're joking."

He shook his head. "Nope."

"What if I told you I missed sucking your dick last night and I want to make up for it?"

His hand jerked, but he said, "Still no."

"Your penis disagrees with you."

"It's a good thing I'm in charge then." He looked down. "Barely," he muttered.

I laughed.

"Just promise me you'll do it," he said in a serious tone. "You deserve to be treated better, Rayne."

He cared about me.

I mean, of course he did. We were friends.

It still made me feel good.

"Okay. I'll do it for you."

He shook his head. "No, babe, you need to do it for you."

I opened my mouth.

"Promise," he warned.

I sighed. "Okay, I will do it for me."

He pointed a finger at me. "I want a full report."

"Whatever."

"Who's in charge, Rayne?"

"*In bed*. Not my personal life."

"I didn't mean like that." He cracked up with a laugh. "I meant, I'm the one in charge of the cock."

Rolling my eyes, I relented. "Fine. I'll let you know what she says."

"Finally." He spread his arms wide. "Then, I'm all yours again."

If only he really were.

No, Rayne. Bad Rayne.

I dramatically stuck out my lower lip. "Too bad I have to get ready for work. We don't have time."

I stole a glance at his erection. It bobbed under the covers, and it made me feel attractive, and I wished I didn't have to work.

"No time for a blow-job lesson, but you don't need them anymore anyway. At least, not every day."

I lifted my gaze. "I don't?"

"You know you don't." He smirked. "You know that you know what you're doing."

I tried to hide my grin. He was right. I knew what I was

doing at this point.

"That doesn't mean I don't want you sucking my dick though. You can still do that whenever you want."

I snickered. "Noted."

"We have time for a quickie though." He slapped his thigh. "Hop up here and ride me, Rayne."

And just like that, I no longer wanted to have sex.

Turning away, I quickly scooted off the bed and said, "No, I don't think we have time. I need to get to the office early."

He snagged my arm and pulled me down onto my back. My head landed on his upper leg, and I was forced to look up at him.

"What's wrong?"

I schooled my face. "Nothing."

"Liar. Tell me."

Ugh. "I don't want to tell you."

"If it involves the two of us in bed, you'd better tell me." He slid his hand down my stomach and in between my legs. "This is mine, remember?"

"Fine. I don't like to be on top, okay? It's my hard no."

Cade blinked down at me. "So, I can tie you up, bite you, and boss you around in bed, but you riding me is off-limits?" Tenderness crossed over his face. "Babe, I'm sure you're not that bad at it."

I laughed. He was so sweet but so clueless.

"No, Cade. It has nothing to do with skill. I don't like the way it makes me feel."

He looked at his hard shaft and back to me. "We can always take it slow. I know I'm big, but—"

With a hand on his cheek and a thumb on his mouth, I stopped him. Because if he kept talking, I might change my mind and get on top of him.

"No. I mean, I don't like the way it makes me feel about myself. I know you find me sexy, and I love that because it makes me feel sexy. But when I'm on top, I feel...big." I closed my eyes. "I hate it. I hate feeling like that, and I hate that I feel like that because there is nothing wrong with being big." I opened my eyes and gritted my teeth. "There is nothing wrong with being fat." Turning my head away, I admitted, "It makes me feel like all the work I've done on myself means nothing, so I'd rather avoid it altogether."

Cade used a finger to slowly turn my head. "How long do we have left together?"

I quickly did the math. "If you count today, twenty days." I wrinkled my nose. "Why?"

"Because I have twenty days to show you that you're just as sexy on top of me as you are under me."

I snorted. "Good luck."

"Baby, I don't need any luck." He grinned, pulled his leg out from under me, and climbed over faster than I could protest. Pushing my hair out of my face with both hands, he said, "I guess we'll have to do this missionary."

"Or doggy," I offered.

"I like the way you think," he said, pulling down my pajama bottoms.

I flipped over and lifted my ass. "Do me a favor and pull out." It would save me cleanup time.

Cade pulled me to the end of the bed and thrust deep inside me. "Never. When I come, I come inside you." He pushed my shoulders down and said, "I want to think about my cum being inside you all day."

TWENTY-ONE
CADE

I COULDN'T STOP THINKING ABOUT WHAT RAYNE HAD told me yesterday morning. It made me frustrated and sad. It also made me very determined to show her how good she could look while riding my cock.

Quickly, I adjusted myself before someone walked into the storage room, looking for me. I was searching for a box of coasters. I was not supposed to be thinking about Rayne and sex.

After a couple more seconds, I found what I was looking for and headed out to the dining room.

"Jana," I called out to the server who had been looking for the coasters. "Found some," I said when she turned around.

My phone rang just as I handed them over to her.

"Hey, Beau," I answered. "Give me a minute so I can get to my office."

Once there, I closed the door.

"What's up?" I checked my watch. "Aren't you at work?"

"Yeah, I'm taking a quick break." He sighed. "How are things really going with the bet? We did a lot of joking around the other night, but I want to seriously talk about it. You have quite a bit of time left. Do you think you can make it the rest of the month?" Beau's tone was heavy. He sounded stressed.

I dropped my ass into my chair. "Things are going well. I'll be honest; when you brought it up, I thought there was no way I'd be able to win. Not happily anyway. But I'm doing great." It helped to have an enthusiastic bed partner who didn't get clingy. "Why do you ask?"

"You know how I love to experiment in the kitchen. I had some spare time yesterday. Wednesdays are usually slow. And I came up with this killer dish. Everyone who tried it loved it. But the owner wouldn't even consider giving it a chance. It just..." He groaned.

"Feels like your talents are being wasted? Feels like you're underappreciated? Feels like they think you don't know what you're doing?"

"All that." He chuckled. "I was going to say something like, *It just felt frustrating,* but I think you nailed it."

"Glad I could help."

"Anyway, I've been scared. The thought of running our own place scares the shit out of me. But I'm so tired of being patted on the head for being a good little chef for only doing what I'm told when I know I can do better."

I smiled. "Damn right."

"I think we should start looking for properties."

My smile morphed into a full-on grin. "Let's do it."

"I'm so ready to quit this place. I'm ready to say forget the bet and just go for it."

That wiped the grin off my face. Done with the bet? I wasn't ready to let Rayne go.

"While I love your enthusiasm, it's going to take us some time to find a place and do everything we need to do to open a restaurant. I can't quit yet. I have bills to pay. And a restaurant to save for."

"Right. That's probably a good reason to stick around for a while."

"Just make sure you save all those recipe ideas for us and stop sharing them for free at work."

"Good thing I have a notebook full of them."

"Music to my ears." I leaned forward on my desk. "Also, about the bet. Neither of us has ever backed out of one before. Not even when you bet I wouldn't hide Mrs. Mann's car on our last day of high school."

Mrs. Mann had been the definition of old and crotchety. No one could understand why she was a teacher since she seemed to hate every student she taught.

Beau hooted with laughter. "She was so mad. She wanted to put you in detention so bad, but she couldn't."

I cracked up at the memory of how red her face had turned. "As an adult now, I feel a little guilty about doing that, but it sure was fucking funny."

"Eh, don't feel bad. It was probably the most excitement she'd felt in a decade."

"And all I got was your super-old PS2. You didn't even play it anymore. You had a PS3." I shook my head. "But I couldn't turn down a bet."

"You still can't."

"True. But neither can you."

"How else am I supposed to prove I'm a manly man?" Beau asked jokingly.

"In that case, I'd better complete this bet. I wouldn't want anyone to think I lost my dick." I also didn't want Rayne to think I wanted to be done with her. "Besides, didn't you say I needed to see this through for Em?"

"Yeah. Em knows I'm frustrated with work, but she's hesitant."

"This will give her time to adjust. Go home tonight, tell her what happened yesterday, and let her know we're going to start looking at locations."

"Good idea."

"Now that we have that settled, I have a question."

"What?"

"Your mom. Does she forget to invite Rayne often?"

Beau clicked his tongue. "Not a lot, but it's happened a few times."

"Man, that's fucked up."

"Yeah."

"Why do you think that is?"

"I don't know. Rayne's always been the easy kid. She went with the flow. She did what my parents asked. Back in high school, she always went where you, Em, and I went.

She always did what we wanted to do. We never asked her what she wanted, and she never complained. And I think my mom forgets sometimes because she just expects Rayne to be there because that's what my sister has always done. But she doesn't live at home, and she can't come to family dinner if she doesn't know about it." He sighed. "Maybe Em and I should make sure Mom says something from now on."

"Fuck that. Your mother needs to remember on her own. I told Rayne she needs to tell your mom how hurt she is."

"You did? When?"

I silently cursed in my head. I didn't want to draw any attention to my relationship with her right now, and I had blown that.

"I messaged her later." I winced at the lie. But I couldn't tell him the truth. "She'd seemed really upset, and I wanted to make sure she was okay."

Please don't ask any more questions.

"Maybe I should tell her to say something to Mom too."

I breathed a sigh of relief.

"You should. And maybe Em should mention it as well."

"I'll talk to her."

Wanting to be off this topic before anything else was revealed, I said, "And let me know when you want to look at some buildings to buy or lease. We should probably find a realtor."

"I know someone. Or rather, Em does. I'll let you know what I find out."

"I'll be waiting."

"I'd better get back to work, but one last question."

"What?"

"Have you been spending every night with the same woman?"

"Almost."

"Holy shit. And you don't feel like you're being smothered?"

I shifted in my seat. "No." *What does that mean?* "But she knows this isn't permanent."

"And you trust her? Even if she's not lying, how do you know she won't change her mind?"

I snorted. "I trust her as much as I do you. And she won't. We've known each other for a long time. She went into this without any expectations."

"Wow. Now, I want to meet her."

I froze.

"I never get to meet your women."

Running my hand through my hair, I said, "There's a good reason for that. If they meet you, they're going to think they're special."

"This one kind of is," Beau argued.

And you already know her.

"Nah, she's not special."

Liar, a voice inside me whispered.

A sudden pinch hit my chest, and I rubbed my sternum.

Wanting this conversation to end, I rapped my knuckles on my desk, hoping he thought it was my door. "I'd better go," I told Beau. "Duty calls."

"Later."

I hung up, rested my head back, and took a few breaths. I was torn. I hated lying to my best friend. But, on the other hand, I really, really liked fucking his sister.

Pushing my dishonesty with Beau to the back of my head, I thought about what he'd said about high school and how she always did what Beau and I wanted to do, and I lifted my phone again.

> Me: I want to take you out on Saturday.

> Rayne: I have Vivian's St. Patrick's Day party on Saturday.

That was right.

> Me: Okay. Friday then?

> Rayne: Tomorrow? But that is the actual holiday. Are you sure you wouldn't rather go out with friends and party?

> Me: What's the point? I'm going home with you, no matter what.

> Rayne: You sure know how to sweep a girl off her feet.

> Me: This is why I don't do relationships.

> Rayne: You don't have to take me out.
> We can hang out at home.

> Me: We do that already. I want to take
> you somewhere.

I wanted Rayne to feel like she wasn't invisible. Like she wasn't a nobody.

> Rayne: Okay. Where are we going?

> Me: You pick. We can do anything you
> want or go anywhere you want.

As long as your brother isn't there.

I wanted her to pick something to do since she'd always had to tag along with us in high school. And even as adults, Beau and I were the ones who'd started the monthly dinner thing. Rayne and Em did it because we did.

> Rayne: I don't know what to suggest. I
> want you to have fun too.

I hated that she felt like she had to please me. Where was the strong lawyer I'd overheard bossing others around?

> Me: Tell me what you like to do on dates.
> And then we'll do that.

> Rayne: Okay, but prepare to be bored. I
> like going to dinner and a movie. I'm an
> easy date.

I laughed.

> Me: Dinner and a movie it is.

> Rayne: And it's going to be a romcom. Don't say you don't like them. I'm sure they aren't your favorite, but they are funny, so I know you'll laugh a little.

There was her backbone.

> Me: *putting my hands up* You'll hear no complaints from me.

I put my phone down and looked forward to Friday.

TWENTY-TWO
CADE

On Friday, Rayne picked a restaurant that neither of us had been to, but she'd always wanted to try it. It was far from where we lived, which was perfect for not running into Beau and Em.

"Beau texted me today and asked what I was doing tonight," Rayne said as she set down her fork.

"Me too."

"What did you tell him?"

Using my napkin, I wiped my mouth. "I told him I had other plans. He didn't say much after." He'd sent back a wink emoji. "What about you?"

"I thought about telling him I wasn't going to do anything since I have a party to go to tomorrow, but then it crossed my mind that they might show up at my house. So, I told them I had a date."

My eyebrows went up at this.

Rayne waved her hands in front of her. "Oh my God, I just said that because it's dinner and a movie. I don't actually think this is a date."

I smiled. "It's fine, Rayne."

She dropped her hands and furrowed her brow. "It is?"

Laughing, I grabbed her hand and squeezed. "Yes. We're doing dinner and watching a movie. It's a classic date."

She grinned and squeezed back.

"Besides, it's you." I shrugged. "It doesn't mean anything."

Her eyes dimmed, and she pulled her hand from mine.

Shit. I'd messed that up.

"I didn't mean it like that." I licked my lips, searching for the right words. "I meant, you won't read too much into this."

"Right. Of course." She picked up her fork again and wouldn't meet my eyes.

"Rayne."

She paused and lifted her gaze.

"You mean something."

I could see she didn't believe me.

"Say it back to me."

"Say what back?"

"That you mean something. I want to hear you say it."

She rolled her eyes.

That was a good sign. She was more annoyed than mad.

"Say it," I repeated. Tilting my head, I added, "Don't make me tell you to take off your panties."

I didn't want the evening to revolve around sex—that would come later—but I was willing to use anything in my arsenal I could.

"Fine. I mean something."

"Thank you."

She leaned forward. "Just a note: threatening me with no underwear isn't really much of a threat."

My cock immediately hardened.

Fuck, this woman.

I almost changed my plans for the night, but I was determined.

"Noted, baby." Breaking eye contact, I leaned back in my seat. "Now, tell me something unsexy, so I don't pull you into the restroom at this fancy restaurant."

Rayne laughed and told me a story about a colleague at work.

We both behaved for the rest of dinner and made it to the movie without incident. I made sure to order popcorn and drinks and picked seats in the middle of the theater. I didn't want her to think I had brought her there to make out like teenagers.

We did go to a romcom, and while I hadn't been excited about seeing it, I was glad it made Rayne happy. And she was right. I did laugh, and by the end of the movie, I was rooting for the main characters to get together.

I held her hand on the drive home. We rode in

comfortable silence, and I liked that we didn't have to constantly find something to talk about.

And when we walked into my house, I slipped her purse from her arm and led her to my room. It reminded me of our first night together, and this was just as exciting as then.

I left the shades open in my room and the lights off. The moon and stars provided just the right amount of luminance for what I had in mind.

Tonight was about her. No bossing her around. No blow jobs. I planned to kiss every inch of her and give her what she wanted.

Starting with her mouth.

I pulled her into my arms and brushed my lips over hers. Patiently, I waited for her to lick the seam of my lips, and when she did, I groaned into her mouth as she deepened our kiss.

She pushed her breasts into my chest, and her tight nipples were like a brand to my skin. When I tore my mouth away, we were both breathing heavy, and I had to stop myself from demanding she strip out of her clothes and bend over so I could fuck her.

I kissed the corner of her mouth and then her collarbone. I continued to pepper kisses down one side of the V-neck front of her dress and back up the other. It wasn't until I reached her shoulder that I went for the zipper in the back. Slowly, I lowered the metal tab, kissing every inch of her skin as it was exposed to me.

When the material pooled at her waist, I moved back

153

up to her bra. With the same painstaking slowness, I removed her bra and kissed her breasts and nipples, barely refraining from tugging her nipples into my mouth.

"I love your breasts," I whispered against her skin and lowered myself to my knees to kiss her belly.

She brought a hand up, but I stopped her with a hand on her wrist.

"Please don't. I love your stomach."

She didn't try to cover herself again.

I continued to undress her, kissing each body part and telling her how much I loved it.

When she was naked, I led her over to the bed and laid her down before stripping off my own clothes. Lying down beside her, I brushed my palm over her body again until her breathing was ragged and hard.

"Cade?"

"Yeah?"

"Touch me."

I smiled. "I am touching you."

"You know what I mean."

"Do you want me to touch you somewhere specific?"

"*Yes*," she hissed.

"Tell me." I traced a finger around her areola and down her abdomen, pausing at her mound.

She blinked up at me.

"Go on. I want to hear the words from you."

"My nipples. My pussy."

I groaned. "And what do you want me to touch you with?"

"Your hands, your fingers, your mouth, your tongue. Your cock."

Nudging her thighs apart, I lowered my lips a hairbreadth from her nipple. "I thought you'd never ask." I sucked the red tip against my tongue and pressed two fingers in her cunt with a thumb on her clit.

Her back bowed off the bed as she exploded on my hand. Her inner walls throbbed around my fingers, even as her body dropped back to the mattress.

Whoever had said this amazing woman was bad in bed was just plain wrong.

I shifted over her closest leg, moving down between her legs.

"What are you doing?"

I chuckled. "I think you can guess, baby."

"Honey, you don't have to go down on me."

I growled against the inside of her thigh. Something about hearing her call me honey did something to me. I wished she would do it more.

"I already came."

"I know. And you're going to again."

"But I want to come with you inside me."

My cock jumped against the bed.

"Don't worry. You will." I swiped my tongue through her folds. "*After* you come in my mouth."

When I finally made my way back up her body, she was boneless with her chest heaving and a soft smile on her face.

I grabbed my dick and brushed the tip through her wetness.

She rubbed her hand over my chest. "I don't think I can come again."

Putting my mouth next to her ear, I whispered, "Yes, you can." As I gradually pushed inside her, I added, "I'm going to make love to you until you do."

And that was exactly what I did.

TWENTY-THREE
RAYNE

"Who all is going to the party tonight?" Cade asked as I folded my dress from last night and placed it in my overnight bag.

"It's Vivian and Dominick's party, so those two, obviously. And Delaney is going to be there. But they are the only people I know." And maybe Vivian's cousin, Hugh, but I didn't really know him, and Vivian had never said if he was going or not.

I looked over my shoulder at Cade. He was lying on his side on the bed with his head resting in his hand. He wore jeans and a sapphire-blue T-shirt that matched his eyes. He looked just as sexy as he had last night in his black dress pants and gray button-up shirt.

My body still tingled from the way he'd made love to me last night. His words, not mine. And while it had been clear from our dinner conversation that he wanted this arrangement between us to be temporary, no man had ever made me feel as beautiful and as special as he had the night before.

For someone who didn't do relationships, he was creating very high standards when it came to me finding my next boyfriend.

I pulled my hair pick from my bag. It was mid-afternoon, but Cade and I had slept in, so I had only gotten dressed after a long shower a few minutes earlier.

"After this month is over, do you think you'd consider putting me on your list of regulars?" I asked as I combed through my wet hair.

"What?"

I turned to face Cade, who was in the middle of sitting up. "I was just thinking that I need to not rush into my next relationship. But a girl has needs, you know." I laughed. Finger combing my hair to make sure I didn't have any tangles, I threw my pick back into my bag. "So, what do you think?"

He had a deep frown on his face. "Are you looking for a boyfriend?"

I chuckled. "Well, not right now. But I don't see myself being single forever." I stepped closer to him and tugged on his shirt. "Unlike some people I know, I like being in a relationship. I like having someone to spend time with and do things with. I understand liking the freedom of being single, but it also gets lonely." I ran my fingers through his hair. "Something you must never get."

"Do you have someone in mind?" he asked, still looking unhappy.

An image of Hugh flashed in my mind. "No." It wasn't a lie. I had only met the guy once, and for all I knew, it might have been the only time. The only reason I was thinking of him was because of Vivian's party tonight.

When he didn't answer, I pressed a thumb between his eyes to get rid of the crinkle there. "Why the frowny face? If you don't want me to be your regular, you can say no. It won't hurt my feelings, if that's what you're worried about." I tapped my chin. "Maybe I should find my own regulars. I have a feeling my vibrators aren't going to cut it after—"

I shrieked in surprise as Cade grabbed me by the hips and threw me on the bed.

Before I could ask him what had come over him, he stripped off my sweater and yoga pants along with my bra and underwear.

He shoved off the bed. "Don't move," he commanded with a pointed finger in my direction and spun around to his closet. After digging for a few seconds, he walked out with something in his hand.

I lifted my head to—

"I said, don't move," he barked.

Someone's in a mood.

He had seemed fine earlier, but maybe he needed to get more sleep.

He grabbed one wrist and then the other and slapped something against each of them. Even though he'd told me not to move, I dared a look and saw soft black handcuffs circling each wrist with the chain threaded through his headboard.

I smirked. "Kinky."

He met my eyes. "Do you have anything to say?"

If he meant our safe word, he was going to be waiting a long time. I didn't know what had gotten into him, but I was fully on board with this ride.

"Have your way with me, sir," I said with a smirk.

He growled and yanked his jeans open. After straddling my chest, he ordered, "Open."

I hadn't given him a blow job in this position yet and definitely not restrained. I licked my lips and opened my mouth.

Pre-cum was leaking from the tip of his dick as he pulled it out of his boxers, and just the sight of his thick length had my core practically dripping.

Cade shifted his stance, bringing his shaft closer, but paused and looked up at my bound hands. "If you need me to stop or pull back, clap." Then, before waiting for my response, he pushed his cock into my mouth.

He moaned, and when I swirled my tongue over his head to catch his essence, he muttered, "Fuck."

Gripping the headboard, he gently began to fuck my mouth. I was ready for him to go full speed, but he took his time before pushing his entire length into my throat. Immediately, he pulled back, but with each new thrust, he held himself there a little bit longer.

When he must have been satisfied that I was okay and

wasn't going to stop him, he let himself go and enjoyed the moment.

In this position and in the middle of a sunny day, I read every little expression on his face, and it was making me so wet that I could feel it on my thighs. I feared the comforter of his bed was soaked.

I hadn't come from giving Cade head without the vibrator, and I didn't think I would be able to, but with each stroke of his shaft, I squeezed my inner muscles, bringing me closer to my own orgasm.

By this time, we were both breathing deep, and I knew Cade was close.

Without thinking, I dropped my knees open and rotated my hips.

Cade yanked his dick from my mouth, reached back, and slapped my pussy.

A sound that was a half-gasp, half-moan burst out of me.

This was new.

I liked it.

"I didn't say you could come."

He didn't often make me wait to orgasm. He was usually demanding that I climax, even when I thought I couldn't.

I clenched my hands into fists, and I didn't say the word that would make him stop.

"Good girl," he said, and I whimpered.

Grabbing his cock, he pushed it between my lips once again and rocked his hips back and forth.

"You know what to do when I come."

I nodded carefully so as not to hit him with my teeth.

Recognizing the sounds he made before he came, I waited for him to slide completely between my lips. But just before he hit his release, he drew his shaft almost all the way out until only the mushroom head remained.

He looked down into my eyes and exploded. His cum sprayed my tongue with the force of his orgasm, and I tasted all of him as I swallowed.

He lowered his lids as his body relaxed. When he opened his eyes again, he moved his body down and over mine.

"You did good, Rayne." He kissed my neck and sucked on the skin on my shoulder until I squirmed under him.

"You're going to leave a mark."

When he lifted his head, he looked down at my collarbone and smirked. "Oops." His tone said the opposite.

He shifted lower and did the same thing to the inside of each breast and both nipples, although the nipple action was purely to turn me on. Traveling south even more, he kissed down my stomach and pushed my legs wide. As with my upper body, he left marks on each of my inner thighs.

I was one big hickey, and I should be mad, but I was so ready for him to fuck me that I was about to beg.

"Please."

Cade parted my lower lips, exposing my clit. His gaze flicked up to mine. "Remember, no coming until I say you can," he warned before lowering his mouth and sucking just as hard on my swollen nub.

My hips shot up—as much as they could with a grown man holding them down—and a low, long moan flew out of me. I was so sensitive there; I almost couldn't handle the pressure. But it also felt so good—too good—and I lowered my pelvis back down, trying to get away.

"Oh my God, I'm going to come. You have to stop. I'm going to come."

Cade pulled away, but only long enough to say, "No, you won't. Not until I say."

The momentary reprieve almost made it worse when he put his mouth back on me. My clit was so swollen that I could feel his tongue with each pull.

My abdominal muscles began to ache as I tried to hold back my orgasm, and just when I didn't think I'd be able to hold it off any longer, he finally stopped.

But he wasn't done completely. Two fingers thrust inside me, directly hitting my G-spot.

"You are evil, and this is torture."

The corner of his mouth tipped up. "But it's only the best kind."

I braced myself for him to continue, but he suddenly froze. He jackknifed off the bed. "Beau."

"Beau?" I cried out. "Shouldn't I be the one to use the safe word?"

He chuckled as he quickly zipped up his pants. "Not the safe word. Your brother. He's here."

"*What*?" I tugged at the cuffs as I realized Cade could

see out the window to the driveway. Thank God my car was in his garage.

He stepped over to me and kissed my forehead. "I'll be back as soon as I get rid of him."

"You can't leave me here like this," I hissed.

He scanned my body. "You're right."

I dropped my head on the pillow in relief.

He dug around in his drawer for what I assumed was the key. But when he straightened, I saw the vibrator he'd bought me.

"You can't be serious," I said.

"Sure am." He quickly moved between my legs. "I have to keep you going until I come back." He paused. "Unless you have something else to say."

I pursed my lips.

"That's what I thought." He snickered and rubbed the tip of my toy between my folds. It didn't take much to get it wet, and he easily pushed it inside me.

He kissed me on the forehead again and picked up his phone from the nightstand. "I'll be back. Make sure to be quiet, or your brother might hear you." When he reached the door, he added, "Remember not to come. And I'll be able to tell if you do." He pulled the door closed and bounded down the stairs.

TWENTY-FOUR
CADE

Beau knocked just as I reached the front door. I swung it open.

"Hey, fucker. What are you doing here? I thought we were getting together tonight."

Normally, I wouldn't care if my best friend dropped by, but when his little sister was tied up and naked in my bed, I wasn't exactly happy to see him.

"Em's parents want to do dinner with the fam—her brother and sister-in-law came into town—but I didn't want to wait to show you the properties the realtor had sent me." He flashed his laptop at me.

"Oh shit." I wanted to see those too.

As I let Beau in, I glanced toward my stairs. A few minutes of looking through some real estate listings wouldn't take too long. It would only make Rayne's orgasm that much better when it happened.

Speaking of which...

As I walked with Beau to my kitchen, I pulled up the app that controlled the vibrator and turned it on to a low setting.

I listened for Rayne to make a noise, wondering if I should have gagged her, but whatever she was doing to keep quiet was working.

Beau set his computer on the kitchen counter and opened the cover.

"You could have emailed them to me," I offered.

"I know. But I wanted to show you in person and let you know what I think."

I couldn't argue with that. "Good point."

We managed to get through the listings in a half hour. There were only four, and two of them were immediate noes.

"I think we need to wait for more or really think about the other two."

Beau closed his laptop. "One other thing."

I shifted from one foot to the other and grabbed my phone to turn off the vibrator. I had been messing with the settings the whole time, but I was feeling guilty and thought she deserved a break.

"What's that?" I asked.

"We could always buy an already-established restaurant that's for sale."

I frowned, ready to tell him, *Hell no.*

My best friend held up his hand. "Just give it a thought. I don't even know if there are any for sale, but we would be able to open for business a lot sooner."

"But you'd be where you are now. Making someone else's recipes."

Rubbing the back of his neck, he sighed. "I know. But I'd be able to add my own at some point."

Seeing that he was stressed, I said, "I will think about it, but I'm not going to give up after four buildings. And you shouldn't either."

He nodded. "You're right. I won't."

I glanced at the clock on the microwave.

Beau chuckled. "Got somewhere to be?"

Yeah. My bedroom.

I lifted a shoulder. "Kind of."

"Shit, man, why didn't you say so?" He picked up his computer. "Sorry about tonight. I was hoping we'd hang this afternoon. But rain check? I haven't seen you much since the bet started."

"Next Saturday. Guys' night."

"Sounds like a plan."

I showed Beau to the door and sprinted up the stairs. Slowly, I pushed open my bedroom door, unsure of what I'd find.

Maybe an angry Rayne. Or worse, a sad Rayne or hurt Rayne because I'd left her handcuffed to my bed and alone for so long.

When she'd started talking earlier about a future boyfriend or fuck buddy—whether real or not—I had been filled with the need to shut her up and show her she was mine. At least, for right now.

I didn't know if I was going to pay the price for letting my emotions get away from me earlier.

But when she came into view, she turned her eyes to me, and they were filled with neither anger nor hurt. They were glassy with desire.

Goddamn, she was perfect for me.

I had wanted to spend more time playing, but I couldn't deny her any longer.

Quickly, I shed my clothes and got on my knees between her legs. I held on to one thigh and gently removed the vibrator. It was coated in her desire, thick and white, showing just how turned on she was.

I threw it on the bed, pulled her hips over my thighs, and slammed into her. With her back on the bed and her hips tilted up, I stroked my cock over her G-spot.

"Baby, whenever you're ready, you can come."

She must have been waiting for me to give her permission because without any warning, she detonated.

Her orgasm was so hard that she forced my dick from her pussy and sprayed me in the chest and face.

I froze, but only for a second before I shoved into her cunt once more.

"Again," I commanded.

It took a few more thrusts this time, but it was worth it when she squirted on me a second time.

Her body shook with the force of her climax, and I needed to feel it again.

Again.

Again.

Again.

Time lost all meaning; the only thing I was aware of was making her come. Just one more time.

One more time.

"Cade, please." Rayne tried to kick me away, but she didn't have the energy for more than a tap. "I can't anymore."

I fell over her and lifted her leg. As I drove my way home, I met her gaze and made sure her eyes were on me until I poured myself deep inside her.

After unlocking the cuffs from Rayne's wrists, I held her as I rubbed her back.

"Are you okay?" I asked.

She sighed and nuzzled my chest with her nose. "I'm great. Although I don't want to do a single thing for the rest of the day now that my bones feel like they've lost all stiffness and my muscles are weak."

Running my hand down her spine, I kissed her forehead. "It wasn't too much?"

"No."

"Good girl." I smiled, and she gave a hum of appreciation. "After today, I see how much your name fits you."

Tilting her chin up, she furrowed her brow. "Why's that?"

"You made it rain all over me and my bed. I have to

change my sheets, and I think the two of us need another shower."

With a groan, she buried her face in my chest. "How embarrassing."

Using a finger, I lifted her face so she could see my eyes. "Stop. It was fucking amazing."

Wondering how often she did it with others, I frowned.

"Please tell me this isn't what your past boyfriends were complaining about." Bunch of prudes, if it had been.

She chuckled. "No. The few times I've ever done that were with myself. Never with a guy."

I growled and drew her tight as I kissed her. My dick grew hard between my legs at the mere mention of being the only man to make her squirt. Especially over and over again.

If I hadn't put her through so much already that afternoon, I would have rolled her onto her back and found my way back inside her.

But she didn't need me shoving my cock into her so soon, so I reluctantly lifted my head.

"I love that I'm the only one," I whispered against her lips. "Thank you."

"You're welcome, honey," she whispered back.

With a groan, I threw my head back against the pillow. She was making it really hard for me to be good.

I needed something to keep my mind off of sex.

"Does this mean you'll stop calling me Rayne Storm when I'm mad?"

Laughing, I said, "First, I rarely call you that anymore.

But when I tell you I'm in the mood for Rayne Showers, you'll know what I mean."

She groaned again.

I looked at her. "We'll just make sure not to tell Beau about your new nickname."

A small snort escaped her. "What did my brother want anyway?" She narrowed her eyes. "Did you know he was coming over?"

"No, I had no idea. We were supposed to hang out tonight, but he's having dinner with Em's parents, her brother, and her sister-in-law. So, he came over to show me the stuff the realtor had sent him."

Her eyes lit up. "I didn't know you were looking. Anything good?"

"Eh. It's okay. We'll see. We're just getting started."

"True." She sat up and swung her legs to the floor. "So, what are you going to do tonight while I'm at the party?"

I shrugged and ran my fingers through Rayne's hair. "Maybe go visit my mom. I haven't seen her in a while."

She turned sideways. "Why's that?"

"You, for one," I joked. "But also, she and her new husband have been traveling a lot."

"Good for her." She looked down. "Can I ask a question without freaking you out?"

My eyebrow lifted. "Not a great way to start, but I'll do my best."

"Do you think you're afraid of commitment because your dad left your mom when you were little?"

She jumped when I laughed.

171

"Okay, not the reaction I was expecting. I thought you were going to read too much into my question and think I wanted to be with you or something."

I smirked. "But you do want to be with me."

She tsked. "You know what I mean."

"You mean, like, a boyfriend-girlfriend sort of thing. But, no, I know you're not trying to change me or hint at something, if that's what you're getting at."

"It is."

"So, Mom is part of the reason I like being single, but not for the reason you think. She never dated or brought guys home the whole time I was growing up, but she was happy. She didn't need to be with anyone to fulfill her or anything."

"She's very independent."

"Mostly, I'm single because I like to be. I like my freedom. I like not being tied down. I like not having to answer to anyone. And my mother showed me that I don't *need* to be in a relationship to be happy."

Rayne nodded in understanding.

"So, I'm not afraid of commitment. I'm more afraid of someone getting the wrong idea about what I want. Because my mom also taught me to treat people with respect and not give false promises, so that's what I try to do." I sighed. "I know I'm blunt sometimes, but it's better to be a little offended by someone you just met than get hurt by someone you've developed feelings for."

"So mature of you."

I snickered. "I also don't like drama, so there's that."

"Ah, there's the rake we all know and love."

"Rake?"

"It's an old-fashioned term."

"What does it mean?"

"It's a nice way of saying manslut."

Grabbing her hand, I yanked her over to me. "Well, this manslut wants to take a shower with you."

"I suppose I can fit that into my schedule," she said with a grin.

TWENTY-FIVE
RAYNE

A CAR PULLED UP NEXT TO MINE IN VIVIAN AND Dominick's apartment complex parking lot, and I waved at Delaney. Since we only knew the host and hostess and each other, we'd made plans to meet before going up to the party.

"Hey, girl," I said after we both got out of our cars. "You look hot."

She was wearing an off-the-shoulder green sweater and stylish jeans.

She rolled her eyes, but I could tell she liked my compliment. "Thanks. You never know; I might meet my future husband here."

I laughed. "For some reason, I thought you never wanted to get married again."

"I'm not in a rush, but I don't want to be alone forever." She eyed me up and down and smiled. "Someone else looks hot tonight."

Pretending to hold a fake skirt, I curtsied. "Thank you."

The invitation had said the dress code was casual and to wear green, so I'd opted for jeans, like Delaney, and a butterfly-sleeved blouse with a lace V-neck, showing a hint of cleavage.

I hadn't thought it was too sexy for a St. Patrick's Day party, but before I left Cade's, he bent me over his couch to have sex one more time. He'd told me he wanted me to go to the party with his cum in me, just to make sure I didn't hook up with anyone else.

It wasn't going to happen, but I hadn't stopped him. The strong feminist in me should have been horrified at his possessiveness, but I liked it. I told myself it was because it was temporary, but I had a feeling it was something I was going to be looking for in a future boyfriend.

Just not too possessive. If he thought he could control me, I'd dump his ass faster than I could say, *Red flag*.

We made our way up to Vivian's floor. We didn't need an apartment number to figure out which one was hers. Loud music could be heard through the door. I worried no one would hear us knock, but Delaney barely put her knuckles to the wood before it was pulled open to a smiling Dominick on the other side.

"Welcome, ladies," he greeted us as we entered. He wore a simple, formfitting green T-shirt with broken-in jeans. He sported a sparkly green plastic top hat on his head and green beads around his neck. "Accessories are to the right," he said, pointing to a folding table with plastic necklaces, hats, headbands, and sunglasses. "And help yourself to the food and drinks." He gestured to the island, covered in a lot of green-colored food.

Vivian pushed through a group of people and ran toward us. Her outfit matched Dominick's, and she wore a grin on her face. She had never dressed so casually, but the biggest surprise was the neon-green three-foot yard glass she had in her hand.

"Holy shit, I think she's drunk," Delaney said in shock.

"You guys," Vivian said in a tone I had never heard from her before. She threw her arms around our necks for a big group hug.

Dominick made a drinking motion behind her back, confirming Delaney's theory.

"I'm so glad you made it." Vivian let go and stumbled back. Thankfully, Dominick caught her with an arm around her waist.

"Apparently, my woman's a lightweight," he said.

Vivian giggled.

Delaney scrambled for her purse. "Why the hell am I not recording this? She's never going to believe us when we tell her."

Dominick grinned. "Don't worry. I already got a video or two."

That didn't stop Delaney from whipping out her phone.

Vivian turned in his arms. "You're so warm." She kissed his neck and groaned. "I need a D appointment, Dominick."

"Not right now."

"Why?" Her free hand slipped between the two of them. "I know you're hard."

This was the first time I had ever seen Dominick blush. I didn't know him that well, but he was very confident. I hadn't thought he had it in him to get embarrassed, and I had to cover my mouth to hide my laugh.

"Sorry," he said to us. "I didn't realize my girlfriend needed a babysitter when drinking." He grabbed her shoulders and swung her around to face us. "Baby, we have guests."

Moving his mouth closer to her ear, he said something we couldn't hear, but it made Vivian grin.

Delaney hit a button on her phone. "I can't wait to show her this the next time we go to lunch."

"You're evil," I told her with a grin. "But, uh, make sure you forward that to me, okay?"

"You got it."

"Would you two mind watching her for a bit?" Dominick asked us.

"Of course not," I said.

"Thank you." He gently slipped the yard glass from her grip. "I'll take that."

Quickly, I threaded my arm through hers, so she wouldn't notice her missing drink. "Help Delaney and me find some drinks, okay?"

———

CADE

Hitting the doorbell, I waited for my mom to answer, feeling awkward.

My whole life, I had lived in the same house, and even after I moved out, I would walk in, unannounced, whenever I came home to see her. When my mom and Bernie had gotten married, she'd sold my childhood home and moved into his house because it was bigger. After, I felt like a guest when I visited her, which was probably why I didn't visit enough.

But it was my stepfather who opened the door. "Cade," he said with a big smile as he stepped back to let me in.

"Hey, Bernie. Mom here?"

"Yeah, she's just on her way down. Come in. Sit."

As far as stepdads went, I got a good one. Bernie's first wife had died about five or so years before he met my mom. He had two daughters, who had also been out of the house when he started dating my mom, but the daughters fully supported their relationship. I didn't know either of my stepsisters very well, but we got along. I really had lucked out. Yet, sometimes, I missed it just being Mom and me even though I didn't live at home any longer.

"Cade," my mother said just as I took a seat on the couch.

I stood and gave her a hug. "Hey, Mom."

"I've missed my boy," she said, smiling. "What brings you here?"

"I haven't seen you in a while, and I was free tonight."

"My baby doesn't have a hot date?" she teased.

I rolled my eyes. "Mom, I'm not your baby anymore. And, no, no hot date."

"You'll always be my baby," she said, squeezing my cheeks.

It was then that I really looked at my mother and Bernie. They weren't dressed up, but they definitely weren't wearing clothes that said they were staying at home for the night. They both smelled good, and my mom had jewelry and makeup on.

Immediate disappointment hit me, but I tried not to show it.

"Oh, hey, were you two going out?"

"We're meeting some friends for dinner," Bernie said.

"Oh shit—"

"*Cade Thomas.*"

"I didn't mean to interrupt."

My mother stared at me with her lips pursed.

"And I'm sorry for swearing."

She patted my chest. "It's fine. We were just about to walk out the door. Do you want to come with us?"

Waving my hands back and forth, I said, "No, no, no. I'm not tagging along. You two go and have fun."

Mom looked sad, and I didn't think it was because I wasn't going with. Just what I needed. My middle-aged mother feeling sorry for me because she had something planned tonight and I didn't.

"We'll get together sometime soon?" Hope filled her eyes.

"Of course. Let me know what works for you."

"How about dinner next Sunday?" She fisted her hands. "Oh shoot. I can't do that day. I have my group. How about the following Sunday?"

That would be my last weekend with Rayne. No, my last *night* because it would be one month that following Monday. But I felt bad, saying no. And it was only dinner. I'd have the rest of the night to spend naked with Rayne.

"Sure. Let's plan on dinner."

She beamed. "I'll cook your favorite."

With a smile, I patted my stomach. "You don't have to, but I always appreciate it."

After giving her a hug and telling her I loved her, I quickly left, so I didn't keep the two of them any longer.

A tightness hit my chest, and I rubbed the area as I started my vehicle. I was happy that my mom had found someone to spend her golden years with. For the first time, I wondered if she had gotten lonely after I moved out. While she'd spent a lot of time raising me, I remembered her having friends while I was growing up. I hadn't been her sole focus, nor had she ever treated me as some weird replacement for a spouse, like some single parents did. But I had to consider if all those years she'd spent alone, even if she was content with life, was because she didn't want to date with me at home.

A movement caught the corner of my eye, and I realized the garage door was going up. I jammed my SUV into reverse, backed out, and shot down the street, the feeling in my sternum still there.

Not only could I be the reason my mother had waited to find a partner, but also, maybe she hadn't been as happy as I thought she was back then.

Normally, I would head to a bar, find some chick, take her home, bang the fuck out of her, and send her on her way. But I'd made this bet. And a promise to Rayne. So, I went home instead.

It was going to be a long night.

TWENTY-SIX
RAYNE

"I'm drunk."

Delaney and I exchanged looks and burst out laughing at Vivian's statement.

We had sat her down at the kitchen island, given her some water, and waited for her to sober up a bit while we sipped our own drinks and snacked on food.

I rubbed her back. "The good news is, you're not as drunk as you were a half hour ago."

She groaned. "I don't remember a half hour ago."

"Exactly," Delaney said.

Vivian looked up at the two of us, standing next to her. "Did I make a fool of myself?"

"For a normal person, no. For you..." I started.

"*Yes*," Delaney finished.

Vivian dropped her head in her hands and groaned again.

Wrapping an arm around her, Delaney said, "Don't

worry too much, Viv. You were cute and fun, and Rayne and I loved seeing you let loose a little."

"This is why I don't drink."

"Maybe just take it a little more slowly," I suggested.

"Or not drink at all." Vivian scanned the room. "Where's Dominick?"

Her question was answered when her boyfriend went to the front door to let in another guest.

Delaney stiffened, I gasped, and Vivian bolted off the stool.

"What the fuck is *he* doing here?" Delaney said in a low voice.

The new guest was Preston St. James III, Delaney's ex-husband.

"Oh my God, I didn't *invite* him," Vivian protested. "He's a *name* partner." She looked down at herself in horror. "I can't let him see me like this. I'll never move up in the company again."

Preston was at the top of the ladder at Benowitz & St. James while Vivian was an associate. She'd recently been promoted, but she was still an associate.

Delaney scoffed. "Preston wouldn't do that. This is a party at your home. You're not working, and you're not out in public. He's not going to hold this against you." She rolled her eyes. "And now, you just made me defend my ex."

I snorted.

"Besides, if he gives you any grief at all, I have some stories I could tell you." The corner of Delaney's mouth tipped up in what could only be described as a wicked smile.

"When did your boyfriend get so chummy with your boss?" I asked as Dominick and Preston laughed at something they were talking about.

"I don't know. He's friends with everyone," Vivian whined.

"Baby," Dominick yelled, "look who showed up."

Vivian lifted a hand and smiled weakly. "Hi, Preston."

Preston's smile faltered when he saw Delaney, but he quickly recovered as he sauntered over. Her ex wasn't what one would call traditionally handsome. He was what a romance novelist would describe as craggy. But he oozed testosterone, and one couldn't help but find him attractive. And even if I hadn't heard Delaney drop tidbits about their former sex life, I wouldn't doubt that the man knew exactly what he was doing in bed.

"Hello, Vivian, Delaney, and..."

"Rayne," I supplied.

The corners of his eyes crinkled. "Right. Rayne. Sorry for forgetting."

I shrugged to let him know it was no big deal. "It's okay. We've only met once."

As if an outside force pulled at him, his eyes landed on his ex-wife. "I didn't realize you'd be here."

He seemed almost apologetic, but Delaney straightened her spine, as if he'd insulted her.

"Vivian and I are friends."

He nodded. "Of course. The two of you are doing the Women in Law project together."

"And I didn't know you'd be here," she accused back.

"Dominick invited me. Don't worry; I'm not staying."

Delaney shoved her long hair over her shoulder. "You don't have to leave on my account."

"I wasn't staying anyway. I have...plans." His eyes swept up and down Delaney, and he turned back to Vivian. "Please tell Dominick thanks for the invitation, but it's probably not wise if I stay."

Vivian nodded. "I will."

"Nice to see you all again."

And with that, Preston left.

"Do you think he's going on a date?" Vivian asked.

I winced. Sometimes, she didn't think before she spoke.

"Don't know; don't care," Delaney responded, chin in the air.

But I had a feeling she did care.

She sighed. "Can we not talk about him anymore? My mom is watching my kid overnight, and I haven't had a night out for a long time. I want to enjoy myself and not think about my ex."

"Of course," I said.

"I'm sorry. Dominick didn't warn me he was coming," Vivian added.

"It's fine. I don't blame you." Delaney walked over to the counter and picked up the bottle of Jack. "Let's do a shot."

Vivian started waving her hands in front of her face but stopped when Delaney raised her eyebrows. "Fine. One. But then I really am done for the night."

With a grin, Delaney grabbed three plastic shot glasses and filled them to the top. "Bottoms up, ladies."

Whiskey was not my favorite hard alcohol, but it was better than the tequila Delaney could have grabbed. Especially on St. Patrick's Day. We each picked up our shots, and I threw mine back, swallowing it all at once.

I hissed as it burned the back of my throat, Vivian coughed, and Delaney grinned.

"That was quite impressive," a deep voice said.

The three of us swung around to see Vivian's cousin standing a few feet away.

"*Hugh.*" Vivian ran around Delaney to hug him. "When did you get here?"

"Just in time to watch you ladies down those shots," he said with a grin.

Vivian turned to face Delaney and me. "You remember my friends from the other day? Delaney and—"

"Rayne." He smiled right at me. "How could I forget?"

Delaney snorted and elbowed me in the side. "You go, girl," she said out of the corner of her mouth.

Ignoring her, I said, "Hi, Hugh. It's nice to see you again."

"You too."

His gaze was still directed at me, and I was feeling very warm inside.

"Do you want something to drink?" Vivian asked, and he finally looked away.

"What do you have?"

As Vivian showed her cousin all the choices, Delaney swung toward me. "So, are you going to hit on that?"

"I don't know."

My immediate thought was of Cade, but while I'd promised to not have sex with anyone else while we were together, there wasn't anything wrong with talking to another man. Especially since Cade wasn't my boyfriend and wasn't going to be around forever. Ignoring the twinge in my chest, I focused on moving on from my own ex sometime soon.

"Maybe," I said with a slow grin.

"Maybe, my ass. I want all the details."

I chuckled. "They won't be very juicy, but I'll tell you everything."

Hugh, with a drink in his hand, came over to my side of the island.

"Hey, Vivian. You haven't given me a tour yet," Delaney said.

Vivian looked from her to me and then to Hugh. With a smile, she said, "Come on. I'll give you one."

Once the two of them gone, I said, "They're purposely leaving us alone together," I warned him in case he didn't know. "This is my first time here, too, yet I wasn't asked if I wanted a tour."

Hugh laughed. "I haven't ever been given one either."

Then, he leaned in close. "But I'm okay with being left alone with you, if you are."

I took a sip of my drink. "I'm more than okay with it."

Hours later, I slipped into bed beside Cade and tried not to wake him.

I had stayed out way later than I had planned, and I almost went home rather than coming back to Cade's, like I'd told him I would.

Not only did I have fun with my friends, but I also spent quite a bit of time with Hugh. He actually seemed like a great guy and was nothing like his cousin. Or rather, he wasn't as uptight as Vivian.

At the end of the night, he'd asked for my phone number. I didn't know if he was going to be my next boyfriend, but it was fun to think he might be the next something in my life.

I giggled at the thought of using everything Cade had taught me on Hugh, and the humor promptly switched to sadness. It was then I realized I might not be as sober as I'd thought I was to drive. *Whoops.* It was too late because I was already here for the night.

A hot body moved closer to me, and a heavy arm went around my waist.

"What's so funny?" His voice was thick with sleep.

I turned in his arms. "Nothing really."

I certainly wasn't going to tell him what I had been

thinking. Even though he didn't want to be tied down, he'd made it pretty clear that, for this month, I was his and his alone.

Running my hand up and down his bare back, I asked, "How was your mom's?"

"Fine."

That didn't sound good.

"Fine?"

"I was there all of ten minutes. She and Bernie had plans."

"So, what did you do the rest of the night? You should have texted me. I would have invited you to the party."

There was just enough light for me to make out the frown on his face.

"And then what? Everyone would have thought we were together or something."

Normally, I would be hurt by this, but this was Cade, and he felt that way about every woman. And something was obviously bugging him, but I doubted he was in the mood to talk about it.

"You're right. Men and women can never be friends. Everyone would have known right away that we were fucking, and the next thing you know, they would have thought we were in love and going to get married."

"When you put it like that—"

"It shows how ridiculous you sound?"

He chuckled. "Yeah. I think your brother showing up unexpectedly freaked me out, considering how close we were to getting caught."

189

Since he hadn't mentioned this earlier today, I called bullshit. Since Cade wasn't my boyfriend, I wasn't going to push to get to the bottom of what was really bothering him. If he wanted to talk, I was here. If he didn't, that was on him.

"None of my friends know Beau, but I get it. It was probably a good thing you didn't come. I didn't really want you there anyway."

A fake gasp came from his side of the bed, and I laughed.

Rolling us over, he draped himself on top of me. "Just for that, I'm going to keep you up a little longer."

"If that's a threat, you need to work on your intimidation skills."

"Nah." He gave me a slow, long kiss. "It's a promise."

TWENTY-SEVEN
CADE

THE NEXT WEEK WENT TOO FAST. I'D THOUGHT, BEING the third week into sleeping with only one woman, I would be bored and itching to move on to someone else.

But I wasn't.

Then again, it probably helped that she never pushed me for a commitment and that she was up for anything I wanted to do in bed. Except for being on top.

"I really wish it were my birthday."

Rayne's head lifted from where she'd been typing away on her laptop on her couch. "Why?" She scrunched up her nose. "Is there something happening that you wish you could go do tonight? Just tell Beau. He owes you after canceling last week. I'm sure he'd be game to do whatever you want."

Later that night, I was going to meet up with my best friend and take him up on the rain check he'd offered me last week when he ditched me to hang out with his in-laws.

But my birthday statement had nothing to do with anything happening in the area tonight.

I lowered my gaze and licked my lips. "If it were my birthday, would you give me whatever I wanted?"

She chuckled. "Yes. Because I already do that." Her eyes flicked to her computer and back to me. "Just give me thirty more minutes."

A slow smile of satisfaction spread across my face. "Good. Because I want you to sit on my face."

She blinked a few times, as if in shock, and then she snapped out of her stupor and swung her legs to the floor. "That would be a no."

Closing her laptop, she stood and headed for the kitchen.

Uncertain of her mood and not wanting her to walk away without talking about it, I snagged her arm as she tried to walk past me. "Rayne, I know you have this hang-up in your head, but I want to help you get past it. I want to show you what you're missing." I had just a little over a week left, and I wasn't going to consider myself the best teacher I could be if I didn't get to show her how much she'd love riding me. And letting me eat her out in that position.

With her lips in a flat line, she huffed. "I can't believe you're even talking about this."

"Why? You know I love your pussy." I rubbed my thumb over her wrist. "If I haven't told you, it's the best I've ever tasted, and I've tasted a—"

"I know, Cade." Her cheeks reddened. "And while I

appreciate that you like that about me, that is not the reason."

"Because you don't like the way it makes you feel? I just told you, I want to help you move past that."

Her brow lifted, and her eyes went wide. "You are infuriating, you know that?"

"She said without any conviction in her voice," I said with a grin.

She was trying not to smile, which was my goal. I wanted her relaxed, so she could realize that being on top might not bother her as much as she thought it would, if she would just give it a try with me.

"If I sit on your face, I will smother you. And normally, that idea horrifies me, but right now, it's looking rather tempting."

I tugged her into my arms, and she squeaked when she landed on my lap. "Then, I will die a happy man. *Here lies Cade Nichols. He died doing what he loved most.*"

Rayne busted out laughing. "You are horrible. Also, I would never be able to look your mother in the eye again."

Sliding her laptop from her arm and putting it on the end table next to me, I nuzzled her ear. "Can I tell you something?"

"If I say no, are you going to tell me anyway?"

"Yes."

"Fine. Tell me then." Her voice was filled with fake annoyance.

"You haven't even noticed that you've been sitting on my lap for about a minute now."

Prepared for her escape, I clamped my arms down when she tried to get up.

"You tricked me, you butthead."

"No. I showed you that I can and *want* to handle all of you."

She stopped struggling, and I thought for sure I had her seeing things my way when her phone rang.

She looked at her smartwatch and pushed at my hands. "It's my brother."

"Shit." I instantly released her.

She picked up her phone from the coffee table, took a deep breath, and answered, "Hello?"

Her eyes ballooned, and she slapped a hand over her mouth. "Oh my God."

I flew out of the chair, wanting to demand what was wrong, but I didn't want Beau to hear me.

Beginning to pace, she said, "Yes, I'll be there as soon as I can." She nodded. "Yes, I will call them to let them know." She stopped. "Beau, I will call our parents too. Please. Go be with Em."

She hit End and looked up at me. "Em was in a car accident."

It felt like the air had been knocked out of me. I hadn't expected her to say that.

"Beau is freaking out—rightfully so—and he can't get ahold of her parents or our parents." She marched toward her purse and yanked out her keys. "I told him I'd meet him at the hospital and make some calls along the way."

I ran after her. "I'm going with you."

Putting up a hand, she shook her head. "No. You aren't at my house, remember? There's no way you'd know Em was in a car accident."

"Are you serious?" I scowled at her. "Em is my friend too." Plus, I didn't want Rayne to have to do this alone.

"Okay. Then, we go in our own cars. Give me a ten-minute head start, and I will tell Beau I called and told you, if he doesn't call you first."

Hands on my hips, I nodded. "Fine. I'll give you five minutes and not a minute more."

RAYNE

In the end, Cade must have given me at least a ten-minute head start because he showed up almost fifteen minutes after me.

"Cade?" Beau squinted over my shoulder from where we stood in the ER waiting room.

I spun around to see Cade jogging toward us.

"What are you doing here?" Beau asked. Scrunching up his nose, he said, "It looks like I'm going to have to give you another rain check."

"Dude, don't even worry about it. And Rayne called me."

My brother looked at me. "You did?"

"I didn't know if you'd remembered to call him in your

panic." I threw up my hands and chuckled awkwardly. "He is your best friend."

Beau flung an arm around me. "Thanks, sis." With his free hand, he pointed at me. "She really is the best. Not only did she get ahold of my parents, but she also found Em's parents, who are on their way."

Cade looked at me. "Yeah, she's pretty great."

My brother frowned.

"Can we see Em?" I asked him before he thought too hard on what Cade had said about me.

"Yes, yes. Go in. She's in room 11. I'm going to call her parents myself. I need to fill them in on what happened." Beau hugged me. "Thanks for calling everyone and for getting here so fast."

"You're welcome, and of course. You're family."

Beau went outside to make his call, and Cade and I went in to see Em.

"Hey, I need to use the restroom. I'll be right there," Cade said.

I nodded and went on to find room 11 quite easily and knocked.

"Come in."

Cracking the door open, I said, "It's Rayne. Are you decent?"

She laughed. "Yes. Come in."

Pushing the door wide, I entered and then left the heavy wood open just a sliver. "Cade had to stop and use the bathroom. But he's here too."

"You're so sweet to come." Em had on a gown on top

but her regular pants for bottoms. She had a scratch on her forehead and a bandage on her hand, but otherwise, she looked like her normal self.

"You're my sister-in-law." I wrinkled my nose. "And to be honest, when Beau called me, I thought you were on your deathbed. It wasn't until I talked to him here at the hospital that he told me you only had minor injuries."

Her eyebrows shot skyward. "Really? Because when he was in here, he seemed to be mostly worried about the car."

Lifting the back of my hand to my mouth, I stifled a laugh.

That was, until Cade came into the room.

"Holy shit, Em," he said, going to the opposite side of the bed from me. "Are you okay?"

"Yes, I'm fine."

Cade picked up her hand in his, and with the other, he ran his thumb over the cut on her head. "That looks painful."

She smiled up at him. "It's not that bad."

He smiled back, and his eyes were filled with something I hadn't ever seen before.

It was love.

Cade had never looked at anyone like that before.

Especially not me.

A crash sounded behind me as pain swept through my lower back. I hadn't even realized I had been slowly backing up until I hit some sort of cart.

"Are you okay?" Em asked, but Cade's face showed surprise, like he'd forgotten I was even there.

Suddenly, my chest hurt as much as my back, and the pit in my stomach was rapidly catching up.

Spinning around, I let my hair fall forward to hide my reaction. I picked up the box of tissues and the clipboard I had knocked off the cart, and I quickly schooled my face.

When I turned to Em and Cade again, I reached for my phone and pulled together a fake frown of concern, as if I had received a text. "Oh. Beau needs me. Will you two be okay?" The laugh that came out of me sounded fake and forced, but it was too late now.

Without waiting for an answer, I ran out of the room and through the ER waiting room to go outside.

Once there, I took some deep, gulping breaths and threw my body back against the side of the building.

I had just learned two things tonight that were going to fuck me over forever.

One, no matter how hard I'd tried not to, I was falling in love with Cade.

And two, he was definitely in love with Em.

TWENTY-EIGHT
RAYNE

DISCOVERING THAT THE GUY YOU HAD FEELINGS FOR had feelings for someone else wasn't ideal when you still had over a week left to sleep with him.

Especially since I was pretty sure Cade didn't know how he felt. He might be a commitment-phobe and anti-relationship, but he wasn't a liar. Except maybe to himself.

But it was clear to me. Cade had taken Em's virginity all those years ago, but then she'd left him for Beau. All this time, Cade said he was happy about being single because his mom had been, but I thought it was an excuse he told himself. I didn't blame him. It would suck to be in love with your best friend's wife, a woman you could never have. Not only would he *never* do that to Beau, but Em was also very much in love with my brother.

Poor Cade didn't stand a chance.

And neither did I.

But I was the queen of unrequited love, starting with

Manny Hobbs in seventh grade, and what was one more guy on the list? I'd been friend-zoned so many times; I should be used to it by now. Cade wouldn't be the first person I liked who didn't like me back, and he wouldn't be the last.

We only had nine more nights together. If I could make it till the end, the bet would be done, our agreement would be over, and I could move on from this whole thing.

Would it hurt? Yes. Cade had warned me not to fall for him, and I'd promised I wouldn't. It would take me a while to get over him, but I would.

And despite my own heart hurting, I thought I hurt more for Cade. He hadn't moved on from Em after all these years, so there was a strong possibility he never would. At least I felt like my love life still had a chance.

"Hey, what are you doing out here?"

I had forgotten Beau had come outside to make a phone call.

Pushing myself away from the side of the building, I said, "I needed some fresh air."

"Is Cade still in with Em?"

I studied his face to see if he had any clue what I had figured out, but he didn't appear to be concerned at all.

"Yeah."

Just then, the ER doors opened, and Cade walked out. "Beau, Em's asking for you. They're getting ready to discharge her. And no one told me her injuries were minor. I made a fool of myself in there."

Poor Cade.

My brother laughed. "Sorry, dude. I panicked when she called me, saying she was in an accident. Turns out, Em fared way better than the car."

"I hope you have good insurance," Cade joked.

Beau groaned. "I don't even want to think about that right now."

"And you don't have to. Focus on your wife," I told him. "Is there anything else you need me to do?" Behind my back, I crossed my fingers, hoping my brother would ask me to do something so I wouldn't have to be alone with Cade. I still needed a moment to collect myself.

"Nah. She cut her head and the back of her hand. She didn't even need stitches. The doctor said she's fine to go to work on Monday if she feels up to it. He warned she might be a little sore, but her head CT and whatever X-rays they took were clear. We're going to head home and take it easy tonight." He slapped Cade on the side of his arm. "Sorry for canceling again. Next weekend?" He chuckled. "I promise, third time's the charm."

Cade's eyes cut to mine, and Beau frowned. I knew Cade was probably thinking it was our last weekend together, but I wished he weren't looking at me like he was asking me what I thought. It was obvious Beau was confused as to why Cade was deferring to me.

Not knowing what else to say, I hesitantly came up with, "I don't have any plans with my brother. You go ahead. Maybe Em and I will do something if she's feeling okay."

"We could all do something together?" Cade suggested.

Was he trying to spend more time with Em?

Pass. I didn't need or want to see that.

"No, you two haven't had time to hang out together lately. Plus, we should let Em decide what she wants to do next weekend since this one is pretty much ruined for her."

Beau's eyebrows smashed together. "How do you know Cade and I haven't hung out a lot lately?"

Shit. I suddenly didn't have a good excuse.

"You literally just said you were canceling on me... again," Cade managed to say in a lighthearted way.

I laughed stiffly. "What he said."

Hitting his forehead with his palm, Beau smiled. "Right. Maybe I'm the one who should get a CT scan of my brain."

"Tell Em not to hesitate to call me if she needs anything," I said.

"Same for me."

It was hard for me not to shoot daggers at Cade. He didn't have to be so obvious about his feelings for Em.

Beau hugged me and fist-bumped Cade. "See you two later."

"Bye."

And then I was alone with Cade.

Tugging on the strap of my purse, I couldn't stop myself from fidgeting. I hated feeling awkward around someone that I never had before. I needed to get out of there. "I'd better head home. I need to finish my work."

Apparently, Cade was oblivious because he smiled down at me. "What are you doing tonight?"

Silently, I cursed the fact that I had told Cade I had turned down a friend who asked me to go for drinks tonight. He would think something was up if I told him I changed my mind all of a sudden.

"You know I'm doing nothing." I held up a finger. "But you also know I was looking forward to a night alone." That was the truth. I'd spent so much time with Cade that I needed some alone time.

He stepped closer, just far enough that we didn't touch, and my dang traitorous body heated up.

I needed to have a serious talk with my hormones.

"Can I come over again? I know you want to be by yourself, but we don't have much time left together." Putting his mouth close to my ear, he said, "And I really want to be inside you tonight."

I closed my eyes and swayed.

I wanted that, too, because he was right. We didn't have much time together, and even if I was going to end up sad when it was over, I needed to remember why I'd initiated this deal with Cade in the first place.

To be better in bed and knock the pants off my next boyfriend.

And there were two things I could do to keep distance between us.

Lock away my feelings and make tonight all about sex.

Opening my eyes, I spun around and ran for my car.

With a quick glance over my shoulder, I watched a shocked Cade standing where I'd left him.

Once I flung the door of my vehicle closed and started it, I sent him a text.

> Me: You can have me when you catch me.

Then, I shoved my car into drive and raced home.

I didn't hit my garage door opener fast enough, and I had to wait in my driveway for it to open. When I pulled in, Cade's SUV was right behind me.

My heart raced, but I actually found myself laughing as I bolted into the house. I almost had the door shut when his big hand stopped it from closing.

I jumped back with a yelp as Cade strode inside, slamming the door behind him. His expression was serious, but I could see the fire in his eyes, and despite what I had learned that afternoon, it didn't take away from how attractive he made me feel.

My back hit the wall as he stalked toward me with fierce determination in his gaze, and it reminded me of the night he had come to my house after the bet was issued. I wanted to feel how I'd felt that night again.

So, I mouthed off. "What are you doing here? I told you I wanted to be alone."

"That's not what your nipples are saying."

He was right. Despite my bra and shirt, I could feel how hard they were.

I lifted my chin. "Doesn't matter. I don't want you to touch me."

He reached me. "Liar." He was so close that I could feel his breath on my lips. "And I bet if I touched your pussy right now, it would be wet for me."

"I don't think—"

His hand went around my throat, and his eyes landed on mine. "No more talking. Let's find out, shall we?"

I nodded, not looking away.

"Take off your pants."

Swallowing hard, I pushed my bottoms off my hips and butt. Since I couldn't move my upper body, I widened my legs and shimmied to get them to fall the rest of the way.

Cade placed his big foot in between my ankles. "Step out."

I pulled each foot from the confines of my pants, and he kicked them off to the side.

"Undo mine."

It took me a second as I fumbled for the front of his jeans since I couldn't look down, but it only heightened my senses, and I felt his hard stomach and thick cock straining behind his zipper. As soon as I had his pants open, I wrapped my palm around his girth.

He grunted and rocked his hips forward and back as I stroked him with my fist.

With his free hand, he lifted my leg under the knee and set it on the table I kept by my door. I was barely tall enough, and my eyes widened as I pictured myself falling to the floor.

"I got you," he murmured and dragged his hand down my thigh to my cleft. He brushed the seam and shoved two fingers inside my pussy.

I cried out and instinctively clamped my inner muscles down.

"So nice. So tight."

I squeezed again, my orgasm already close.

Ripping his hand away, he growled, "I don't think so. For the rest of the week, you don't come unless my dick is inside your cunt. No coming from sucking me off and no coming when I eat your pussy." He smiled wickedly. "Unless you ride my face."

"You bastard," I whispered.

"But I'm your bastard," he said, sliding his shaft through my folds and thrusting inside me.

My heart squeezed at his words, and I held tightly to his sides as he worked me over, stroke after stroke. My leg began to shake, and my eyes slid closed.

His hand tightened on my throat. "Eyes on me, Rayne."

Forcing them wide, I stared at him as he continued to pound into me until the pressure built and I couldn't take it anymore.

"I want you to come, baby. All over my cock. Soak me."

Crying out, I detonated, shaking so hard that I almost lost my footing. Cade released my neck to wrap his arms around me as he drove in deep one last time, spilling inside me.

My goal to make the rest of the month about sex had

already failed because I felt more connected to him than ever.

So, on Tuesday, when I received a call from Hugh, asking if I wanted to go on a date this coming weekend, I said yes.

TWENTY-NINE
CADE

Shoving my arm under my head, I looked over at Beau from my spot where I was sprawled out on his couch.

"Where did Em and Rayne go tonight?" I pried, hoping to sound casual.

Rayne had been acting differently the past week. She'd been initiating sex left and right with me, and while I enjoyed it—I was a healthy man—it struck me that she was using sex to avoid something. When I asked her about it, she told me it was because her lessons were almost over and she wanted to get the most out of them, but I didn't quite buy it.

Something had changed, but I couldn't figure out what it was. And I was running short on time to find out.

I was hoping a night with Em would make her feel better.

Beau didn't even look away from the TV when he said, "Em is at dinner with her friends, and Rayne is on a date."

What?!

I counted to five so I wouldn't accidentally yell when I asked, "Rayne is on a date? I thought she was with Em tonight."

She hadn't said anything to me about going on a fucking date. She'd just let me assume she was hanging with Em after we talked about it at the hospital. It seemed she'd forgotten the part of our deal where she was *mine*.

"Em asked, but she said no. I guess a friend set her up with him."

She also hadn't mentioned that a friend even wanted to set her up with someone. I was furious, and I had to bite my tongue so I didn't ask more questions. The last thing I needed was for Beau to be suspicious.

I grabbed my phone from where I had set it on the coffee table.

> Me: Where the fuck are you? And don't say with Em. I know you're not with her.

> Rayne: I wasn't going to. You assumed I was hanging with Em, but you never asked.

> Me: You also didn't correct me. Now, tell me where the fuck you are.

> Rayne: If you must know, I'm on a date.

> Me: What the fuck, Rayne? You promised you were mine for the month.

Rayne: No, I promised my pussy and my body were yours. I'm not going to have sex with him. And the month is almost over. I have to start dating sometime.

Me: Yeah. AFTER Sunday.

Rayne: Too late. I'm already here.

The urge to find her so I could throw her over my lap and spank her ass until it was red was strong. Never in my life had I wanted to punish a woman so badly.

Me: Where is here?

Three dots formed but went away. It happened again, and I pictured her getting sidetracked by some handsome guy.

But when the message popped up, I realized why she'd taken so long to text me.

Rayne: He took me to Iron House.

RAYNE

Hugh laughed at something he'd said, and I felt awful for not listening. Despite my feelings for Cade, I had really wanted to give this date a chance. And I might have if, ten minutes in, the very man who haunted my thoughts hadn't texted me.

So as not to be rude, I had excused myself to use the ladies' room while I messaged Cade. But I had to come back after I told him I was eating at his restaurant. If I had waited any longer, Hugh would have thought I drowned in the toilet. Or worse.

But it didn't matter because Cade hadn't answered. Even though my smartwatch would vibrate if I had an incoming text, I couldn't stop peeking at it under the tablecloth.

Which made me a real shit. I should have waited one more week for this date instead of trying to force myself to forget about a man who I was going to see later tonight anyway.

A heaviness fell over me. I thought I was more fucked up now than I had been a month ago.

"Hey, are you okay?" Hugh asked.

Oh jeez, there was no good way of answering that.

Finally, my watch buzzed on my wrist.

> Cade: Tell your date you have to go to the restroom.

If I did that, he really was going to think something was wrong.

> Cade: Don't try me on this, Rayne.

"I think I need to use the restroom again. I apologize."

Hugh sat back in his chair, surprised, but I didn't wait for him to answer. I grabbed my purse and headed toward the restrooms at the back of the restaurant.

Once I was out of Hugh's sight, I pulled out my phone, ready to text Cade to tell him I was doing what he'd asked, when the office door opened. I yelped as a hand pulled me inside.

My phone and purse were ripped from my hands, and I was spun around so my front hit the office door. The room was dark, but I would recognize the hard body plastered against me anywhere.

"Oh my God, what are you—"

Cade sucked on the skin at my neck, making my knees buckle. "I came here to remind you that you are mine." Two hands went under my skirt and straight for my underwear. "You're lucky you're wearing these around him." Pushing them halfway down my legs, he flipped the back of my skirt up and slammed inside me. "Soaked. Just for me."

"I'm not yours," I hissed, mad at him for accosting me during my date. "Fucking me for a month doesn't make me yours, especially when that month is almost over."

"Don't test me."

"And maybe I'm not wet for you," I taunted.

A snarl tore out of him. Cade's fingers dug into my hips, and he pulled completely out of me, then rammed himself back in. And with a thrust of his hips on each word, he growled, "The fuck you aren't."

He was acting like a man possessed. I should stop him

—I knew I should—but with every stroke, I grew wetter and wetter.

"Mine, Rayne. This pussy is mine." He slipped a hand in the V of my blouse. "These breasts are mine." Pulling on my nipple, he twisted it. "These nipples are mine. You know how I know this?" Putting his mouth to my ear, he said, "Every time I claim a part of you, your cunt gets tighter. You like being mine, Rayne. You love it."

God help me, I did.

But I knew I couldn't give in. If I did, he really would claim a piece of me, and I feared I would never get it back.

I shook my head. "No."

"Yes. Everything on you belongs to me. And I can prove it."

"N—"

Cade bit down on my neck, and I couldn't fight it. I burst into a million little pieces that would never be put back together the same way again.

His cock pulsed inside me, each pump filling me with a piece of him.

Unsure of how long we stood there, I suddenly became aware of his hand on my mouth and his body holding up mine against the door.

My body flushed with embarrassment of what his employees had probably heard on the other side and for leaving my date sitting alone at our table.

Disgusted with myself, I shook off Cade, but he didn't seem to care. I was outraged.

He withdrew from my body, only fueling my anger

because of how empty I felt without him inside me. He straightened my top, pulled up my underwear, and spun me around.

"You're going to go out there and end this date. Meanwhile, I'll order a ride for you, and then you're going to go back to my house and get naked and wait for me in my bed until I get there."

I straightened my spine. "The hell I will."

"You made me a promise, and you cheated on our agreement by going on this date, Rayne. Not me. So, unless you want me to invite your date back here so I can show him how full your cunt is with my seed, I suggest you do what I said."

I gasped. "You wouldn't. He has nothing to do with what's going on with you and me."

Cade was one of the nicest guys I knew. I couldn't imagine him being that much of an asshole to some stranger.

"Do you really want to find out if I'm lying or not?"

"No," I admitted.

He stepped forward and kissed me on the temple. "Then, please just do what I said."

When I moved away, my purse and phone were thrust back into my arms. When he opened the door, I walked out, feeling completely defeated.

I made a detour to the restroom, and I was glad I did. My makeup was smeared, and I had to pull the pins out of my updo to hide the bite on my neck. I couldn't believe I had fought Cade on ending my date with Hugh because there was no way I could pretend everything was normal.

My mind and body had been put through the wringer.

Looking as presentable as possible, I found Hugh.

"Oh my God, are you okay?" He leaned forward. "You were in the restroom for a long time."

My face heated. He would probably never want to go out with me again because he thought I had intestinal issues.

But I supposed that was better than him finding out what I had actually done.

"Uh, no, I'm not. I'm so sorry, but I have to cut this date short. I've ordered a ride, and it should be here soon."

Hugh stood, sympathy in his eyes.

It only made me feel like more of an asshole.

"Please. We can reschedule when you're feeling better." He held out his hand. "And, hey, we never made it past drinks. We won't even count this as our first date."

I almost burst into tears at how sweet he was being to me.

"I'm sorry again," I muttered and ran out of the restaurant to where a car waited out front to take me to Cade's.

The next morning, I lay on my back, staring at the ceiling. Cade slept beside me, oblivious to the turmoil going on in my head.

I had toughed out this last week, knowing how he felt about Em. But I had ended up putting his needs before my own.

It wasn't that I didn't love being with him—because I did. But after last night, I realized something significant. Even if this month made him change his mind about dating and commitment and me, it wouldn't change the fact that I would be the woman he fucked and Em would be the woman he loved.

In his dark office, in all his *mine* talk, he never once said, *Your heart is mine.*

And that told me everything I needed to know.

Even though he had come home soon after me and simply held me until I fell asleep, I couldn't confuse his caring for me as anything more than that. Caring wasn't love.

With a hand on his shoulder, I shook him. "Cade."

He sucked in a deep breath and rolled over. He smiled when he saw me. "Hey."

"Hey." I looked away.

"What's wrong?"

"I'm going home."

His brow furrowed.

"And you're going to stay here."

"Why?"

"Tomorrow marks one month. I know it's our last

night, but I have to go." I tried to smile. "Besides, you're going to your mom's for dinner tonight anyway."

My attempt to lighten things didn't work.

"We already talked about this. You promised me a whole month."

His voice was low and almost sad. Not full of anger, like last night. It almost had me giving in.

"Please, Cade, if you are truly my friend, you will let me go."

He sat up. "Will you be at dinner on Friday? We're supposed to celebrate me winning the bet."

"Maybe." I hadn't decided yet.

He smiled. "I hope you come."

I slipped from his bed and kissed him. "Thank you for everything."

He grabbed my hand, stopping me from standing up. "No, baby. Thank you."

Hearing him call me baby was going to be my undoing.

"I have to go," I whispered through a tight throat.

Nodding, he released my hand.

And just like that, the C agreement was over.

THIRTY
CADE

"C*ADE*."

I jerked up from the menu and looked at my best friend. "Sorry. What?"

Sighing, Beau held up two real estate listings. "Which one is better?"

"The one in Eden Prairie. It has more square footage."

"Smart thinking. But I'm going to put them both in the Maybe pile."

I laughed and threw up my hands. "Why'd you even ask?"

"Because you were off in some dream world and I had to do something to snap you out of it."

I scoffed. "No, I wasn't."

I had just been thinking about his sister. When she'd left last weekend, I felt like she had taken something from me with her. It was such a ridiculous thought, but I'd been unsettled ever since.

Not to mention, I hadn't had sex for almost a whole week. Six days, to be exact, and that wasn't like me.

But the only one I wanted was Rayne.

"Sure seemed like it," Beau said.

"Just have a lot on my mind," I muttered.

"Like the—"

"Cade? Cade Nichols? Is that you?"

Over Beau's shoulder, I saw one of the women I used to regularly sleep with saunter toward us.

When my best friend saw her, he raised his eyebrows in my direction, as if to say, *Who is this?*

I cleared my throat. "Hey, Leila. This is my friend Beau."

Leila held out a well-manicured hand. "Nice to meet you, Beau. You are almost as handsome as your friend."

I couldn't be sure with the lighting, but I thought he was blushing.

Leila was very straightforward and didn't waste time with semantics. She went for exactly what she wanted, which was why I had her number. She liked sex as much as me but wanted nothing more. She was the owner and CEO of her own company, and she'd told me she didn't have time for relationships, nor did she want to make time. Her company was her first and only love.

"He's married, Leila."

She smacked her lips in disappointment. "Damn. I could always use another man who knows what he's doing in the bedroom for my roster."

Beau looked stunned but laughed.

"Leila and I occasionally get together to...you know," I finished since we were in the middle of a restaurant.

"Used to get together." She put a hand on her hip. "I haven't heard from you since you canceled on me, like, four weeks ago."

"Yeah, something came up," was all the explanation I was going to give her because I didn't owe her any, but my best friend opened his big mouth.

With a grin, he told Leila, "That's because I made a bet with him that he could only have sex with one woman for a month."

Leila clapped her hands together as she burst out laughing. "That is hilarious." She looked me up and down. "And how is that going for you?" She lifted a brow. "You haven't called me, so it must be going well?"

"Very well. He's done," Beau answered. "Monday was one month, so tonight, we're celebrating."

She pointed at him. "You bet him he couldn't last a month, and he won the bet, but you're both celebrating?"

"I told Cade if he could make it, we'd open a restaurant together."

"Congratulations. You'll have to hit me up once it opens. I have a lot of customers I can send your way."

"Thanks, Leila," I said.

She put a finger to my chest. "Now that you're free again, you'll have to call me."

Not that long ago, I wouldn't have hesitated to say yes, but now, her flirting did nothing to me. Not even a stir from down below.

One month with Rayne, and it occurred to me that I might be broken.

"I'll do that." The words coming out of my mouth felt like a lie.

"I look forward to it. It was nice seeing you again, Cade." With a kiss on my cheek, she was gone.

"She's beautiful," Beau said.

"She is. And very successful. If she really suggests our restaurant to people, we will be very lucky."

"You'd better call her then to keep her happy."

"Eh," I said with a lift of my shoulder.

"Who are you, and what have you done with my best friend?"

Your sister's ruined me, I thought as Em approached our table.

"Hey, Cade." She sat down next to Beau and kissed him. "Hey, hon."

A jealous feeling came over me. Not because I wanted Em, but because I was actually envious of what the two of them shared.

Where in the hell had this come from? I was *never* jealous.

"You missed it," Beau said to his wife. "I just met one of Cade's regulars."

"Shut up." Em's mouth hung open. "And I missed her?"

"Yeah."

"Dammit."

"You two are not funny," I told them.

"You know what's really funny?" Beau asked, all humor gone from his face.

Something told me not to answer.

"What's funny, hon?" Em asked for me.

"Remember the night we made the bet and the woman texted Cade about their plans that night?" Beau was talking strictly to Em, but I knew his words were for me.

I sat back as a sinking feeling came over me. I felt like I was missing something, but I couldn't figure out what.

"How could I forget?" Em said.

"Well, when Cade called me later, I asked him if the woman who had messaged him was the woman he was seeing for the month, and he said yes."

I closed my eyes as the conversation came back to me. I thought I had actually said something less concrete, like, "Yeah. Sure," but it was an affirmative answer all the same. At the time, I had done it to get him not to pry further.

"So, that night, when he had gotten that text at dinner, I'd happened to see the name on the screen. And wouldn't you know, it was the same name of the woman I just met a little bit ago? Only she hasn't seen Cade in a month."

Shit, shit, shit. I couldn't believe that tonight, of all nights, we had run into Leila.

"Do you think Cade slept with her and then someone else during the bet?" Em asked.

"Nope. Because this woman said something about Cade canceling on her."

I was so screwed.

"Uh-oh," Em said and looked at me.

Beau slowly faced me, too, anger filling his eyes. "So, Cade, if you haven't been with Leila, *who the hell* have you been fucking this past month?"

THIRTY-ONE

RAYNE

Leaning against my kitchen counter, I picked at my sad meal. It only reminded me that I was supposed to be celebrating the end of the bet and the beginning of the restaurant. But I hadn't had it in me to have dinner with everyone tonight.

I missed Cade. All week, he had filled my thoughts, no matter how hard I tried to not think about him. Seeing him again so soon wouldn't help me get over him. I needed more time.

Throwing my fork down, I gave up trying to eat when my phone rang.

When I saw it was Em, I almost didn't answer, but the potential guilt of hitting Ignore had me relenting.

"Hello?"

"Rayne, you need to get over to Cade's and talk to him immediately."

My body jerked. "Why?"

"Beau asked Cade who he had sex with during the bet, and Cade wouldn't tell him. Then, Beau told Cade he'd have to forfeit if he didn't reveal her name and there wouldn't be a restaurant. Cade's response was to storm out, and now, Beau's pissed too."

"What?"

There was no way Cade would do that.

"Cade is literally throwing his dream away, and he and Beau are fighting." Em sighed. "I know I was scared about them opening up a restaurant, but Beau brought me around, and he's been excited to do his own thing. Really excited. And I absolutely hate that the two of them aren't talking."

"But why are you calling me?" I asked.

"Rayne, Beau knows Cade's been sleeping with you."

I gasped.

"Okay, he doesn't know one hundred percent, but the two of you have been acting strange lately, and then they ran into this woman. She was the one Cade was going to hook up with the night Beau issued the bet, and Cade let Beau believe she was his partner this past month. Only the woman mentioned she hadn't seen Cade for a while. Beau's suspicion was basically confirmed when Cade refused to say who he'd been with."

"Holy shit."

"Yeah, so get your ass over to his house and tell him not to throw away this opportunity."

I pounded on Cade's front door and paced back and forth. I knew his garage code, and just a few days ago, I would have walked in, unannounced. But it felt wrong now that we weren't sleeping together anymore.

Heavy footsteps moved closer to the door before it swung open to reveal a scowling Cade.

Surprise flashed across his face, but I didn't wait for him to invite me in.

I barreled past him and shouted, "What in the hell were you thinking?"

He let the door swing shut and crossed his arms over his chest. "What are you talking about?"

"Em called me." I waved my arms around. "You and Beau got into a fight. You forfeited the bet. You lost the restaurant." Fisting my hands, I demanded, "What were you thinking, Cade? Everything we did, it was for nothing."

I had ended up sacrificing my fucking heart for his dream, and he'd just thrown it away.

He flinched and dropped his hands. "Nothing, huh?" He lifted his chin. "Fuck you, Rayne." He marched past me. "You can see yourself out."

I ran after him and grabbed on to his bicep. "I'm sorry. Cade, I didn't mean what we had was nothing. But this restaurant was the whole goal."

He stopped walking, but he didn't look at me, so I rounded his front and fisted his shirt.

"I don't understand. You've wanted this forever. Why would you give up like that?"

"For you."

I stepped back. "Me?" I shook my head. "But I want this for you."

"At the expense of you losing your relationship with your brother?"

My hand went to my throat.

"He's been telling you to stay away from me for forever. What do you think he would have done if I had told him I'd been fucking his little sister behind his back?"

"Been mad at you," I said in a low voice.

Cade snorted. "No shit. But he would have been mad at you too."

Hesitantly, I moved closer to him again. "But he would have been way angrier with you."

"Yeah, well, this was not my secret to tell." His big hand smacked his chest. "It's *our* secret. And it would have been really shitty of me to tell him about our relationship without talking to you first."

And that was the moment I went from falling for Cade to being head over heels in love with him.

He pushed my hair behind my ear as his eyes grew soft. "Besides, it's not really any of his business who either of us sleeps with. You and I are both adults, and if we want to be together, we don't need his permission."

My eyes darted across his face, trying to read every inch. "I don't understand."

"I want to be with you, Rayne. Not because of some bet. Not for a month. I want to be with you for real."

"But what about Em?"

Cade's nose curled up. "What the fuck does Em have to do with us?"

I forced myself to look away. "I know you love her."

"What are—"

I put a finger to his lips. "Give me a minute. I saw the way you looked at her after the accident. You were so worried and scared. I've never seen you look at anyone like that. And you took Em's virginity. As much as I rant about it being a social construct and how purity culture ruins everything, it still had to mean something. And then, when she broke up with you, I think it hurt you more than you want to admit. So, you use your mom being single when you were growing up as an excuse for why you are the way you are, but it's really because you can't have the woman you love."

Taking my hand from his mouth, he said, "Are you sure you're not a storyteller instead of a lawyer? Because that's quite the tale you've spun in your head." He cupped my face. "I have never loved Em. What you saw at the hospital was because I heard my good friend had been in an accident. I didn't know if she was going to live or die at that point because no one had told me her injuries were minor and she was going home within the hour. As for in high school, I'd thought she was hot, and I wanted to get in her pants, but I was sixteen. I wanted to get into pretty much every female's pants. It was a one-time thing, and it hadn't even been that good." He smirked. "You probably don't want to hear this, but I slept with someone else the very next night."

"So romantic," I said dryly.

Pulling me into his arms, he said, "Hey, this grand romance was all in your head."

"True."

"So, now that we've established I am not and never have been in love with Em, can I tell you who I'm actually in love with?"

"Who?" I whispered.

A slow smile spread across his face. "You, baby."

I blinked a couple of times because the look in his eyes was ten times stronger than what it had been at the hospital.

"But why didn't you tell me?"

He shrugged. "I've never been in love before. I didn't recognize the signs. It wasn't until your brother confronted me that I realized I couldn't throw you under the bus, not even to get my dream restaurant."

"Even though he's now mad at you?"

Cade chuckled. "He'll get over it. I mean, he got over the Em thing. And I know how badly he wants Blaze to happen. But all that was my risk to take. I didn't have the right to make that decision for you."

"I have to tell you something."

"What's that?"

"I love you too."

He threw his head back and laughed. "For years, I thought those were the last words I wanted to hear, but I love the sound of them, coming out of your mouth."

"So, I guess this means I'd better tell Hugh there'll be no do-over on our date."

Cade's face grew dark, and he growled.

Squeezing his shoulders, I brushed my lips over his. "I'm kidding. You're the only one I want to be with."

"Looking back, Saturday should have been a big fucking clue on how I felt about you." Sliding his hand into my hair, he fisted it as the other went around the front of my neck. "You're mine, Rayne. Every single inch of you. Do you understand?"

"Maybe. I have a question for you first."

His brow rose as he loosened his hold on me. "Oh, really?"

"You said, back in high school, you pretty much wanted to get into any female's…"

What was I doing? This hot man had told me he loved me, and I was going to ruin it.

Cade grinned. "The answer's yes, babe."

"What?"

"Did I want to fuck you back in high school? Hell yeah, I did."

My mouth dropped open.

"But, like, you were an underclassman, and I, like, totally couldn't be seen with you," he said in a Valley Girl voice. In his normal voice, he added, "And then there was Beau."

I couldn't stop the grin from forming on my face.

"So, what do you say? Are you mine, Rayne?"

I nodded. "I'm yours."

"Good. Because I'm yours." Lifting my hand, he placed it on his chest. "Especially my heart."

And what do you know? It felt a lot more special for him to give me his heart than for him to claim mine.

I kissed him, but I quickly pulled away before we ended up naked.

"One more thing."

He groaned. "What?"

"We're going to see Beau and tell him the truth. You are going to get that damn restaurant."

CADE

With Rayne's hand in mine, I waited for Beau to come to the door. The energy was palpable around us as we worried about what her brother was going to say.

When he and Em answered, I said, "I slept with Rayne for the entire month of the bet." Turning my head, I looked down at her. "She can verify we spent every night together."

"Every night?" Em asked.

I looked back to my friends. "Every night." With a lift of a shoulder, I met my best friend's eyes. "What can I say? She makes it impossible not to fall in love with her."

Beau's lips twitched. I knew him well enough to know he was trying to stay mad even though he wasn't.

"You asshole. You weren't supposed to come here and tell me you love her."

Em grabbed his arm and beamed. "I'm so happy for you two." She gasped. "Now, when the four of us go out, it will be true double dates."

"We're not going to be going out for a long time, Em," Beau told her.

"Why not?" She frowned as Rayne squeezed my hand.

My best friend smiled at me. "Because we have a restaurant to save up for."

EPILOGUE

RAYNE

"Knock, knock."

Lifting my eyes from my phone, I saw my handsome, sexy boyfriend standing in the doorway of my office.

"Oh man, is it that time already?" I double-checked the display on my mobile.

Cade walked into the room, his hands behind his back. "It is. Are you ready to go?"

He was meeting Vivian and Delaney tonight. When I'd messaged Vivian and told her I wouldn't be seeing her cousin again and why, she'd demanded we get together.

I typed my last few words and hit Send. With a smirk, I told him, "I was just texting my mom back after she asked me to come over for dinner on Monday."

He leaned over and kissed my lips. "Did you say yes?"

"No. I asked if she accidentally messaged the wrong person since she usually forgets to invite me to family events."

Cade gave me a disappointed look, but he was also trying not to laugh.

"I'm kidding. She already knows how I feel about that whole thing."

"I'm glad you finally talked to her."

"I had to when you *refused* to have sex with me until I did."

He shrugged. "I warned you."

I sighed. "That you did."

"So, what did you really say?"

Rolling my eyes, I said, "I told her we'd be there."

"I like that you included me."

"Always."

Cade went over to close the door, and when he came back, he walked around to my side of the desk. He had a more serious look on his face.

"Before we meet your friends for dinner, I have something for you."

I grinned. "Is that a present you're hiding behind your back?"

Bringing one hand around, he cupped my chin. "It is. But first, I need you to get down on your knees for me."

We didn't have a lot of time before our dinner reservation, but I also couldn't tell Cade no. Besides, someone would show up on time to get our table. We could be a few minutes late.

Slowly, I lowered myself to the floor and looked up at my new boyfriend to see what he wanted from me next.

"Baby..."

"Yeah, honey?"

He brushed his thumb over my lips, then trailed the backs of his fingers down my neck.

My insides clenched, and I shivered at his touch.

"You know I like control in the bedroom."

I nodded.

"I never thought I would meet someone who would accept me the way I was and someone I wouldn't get bored with. Turns out, I already knew her. You are perfect for me, Rayne. And because you gave yourself to me last night, I have something for you. Good girls deserve good things, and, baby, you are a very good girl."

Heat swept through my body. Last night, I'd wanted to give Cade the thing he'd been asking for. I had him lie on the bed, and I got on top of him. Most people probably wouldn't consider that position to be giving themselves to their partners, but he had known how big of a deal it was for me.

"I didn't do it because I wanted something from you. I did it because I love you and trust you," I told him.

He smiled. "I'd been thinking about this for a while. Last night just solidified how perfect it would be."

"Okay."

"With this gift comes an important question."

Immediately, my mind jumped to a marriage proposal. Not many gifts came with an important question. But I was the one on my knees, not Cade, and our relationship was far too new for an engagement.

"I'm ready," I told him.

The hand still behind his back came around, and in it was a suede jewelry box. But I was right. It definitely wasn't a ring.

It was a necklace box.

"Go ahead," Cade urged.

Uncertain of what I'd find, I took the jewelry box and carefully opened it. It was a silver chain with a circle dangling from the center, which was a gorgeous, almost Celtic design.

"It's beautiful, but I don't understand what's so important about it."

"It's not your average necklace. Look at the clasp."

I studied the back and could see where the two sides separated, but, "It doesn't have one."

"That's because it's a lock."

My eyes flicked up to his.

Cade ran a finger over my collarbone around the front of my neck. "It's a submissive collar, and this"—he tugged on the circle—"is an O ring."

The air was pulled from my lungs, and I was at a loss for words.

"Have you ever seen a submissive collar before?"

Nodding, I licked my dry lips. "Yes. But not in real life. And they've always been leather and tight around the neck, like a choker. This doesn't look like it's a choker."

"It's not. It's technically a day collar, and it will lie on you like a necklace. It's more discreet." He picked up the necklace. "If you'll let me, I would like to put this collar on

236

you and lock it." He lifted my chin. "But it will mean you are truly mine."

"Can I take it off?"

"Technically, yes. It's not a permanent lock, but it's safe to shower and sleep in." His expression turned serious. "If you put it on, Rayne, you won't be taking it off. Do you understand?"

I nodded.

"Can I put this on you?" His voice was low, as if he was worried I would say no.

"Yes."

A grin split across his face, and he removed the necklace I had worn that day and replaced it with his collar.

Cade held out his hand and helped me stand. "Now, you're mine."

"I already was," I reminded him.

He shook his head, as if he couldn't believe how lucky he was. At least, that was what I hoped he was thinking.

"You look beautiful. I can't wait to get you naked and see you only wearing my collar and my cum." He yanked me into his arms and took my mouth until we were both breathless. "Are you sure we can't just go home?" He peppered my neck with kisses.

I squirmed in his arms. "Unless you're going to command me to, we're going to dinner with my friends."

My skin vibrated with the force of his groan.

"I'm half-tempted to do just that." He drew in a big breath, lifted his head, and released it. "But I know how much you want to go tonight."

I fingered my necklace. The O ring sat just below my collarbone. "Is everyone going to know what this means?"

"I'm sure a few will, but they won't judge. Most people won't have a clue. That's why I picked this style. I don't want to embarrass you. I just want you to know who you belong to."

"You."

"Damn right it's me."

Wrapping my arms over his shoulders, I said, "Thank you."

"No, baby. Thank you." He smacked my ass. "Let's get out of here and go see your friends."

Grabbing my boyfriend's hand, I let him lead me out of my office with a grin on my face.

I wasn't a betting person, like Cade was, but I would always bet on our relationship going the distance.

TURN THE PAGE FOR A SAMPLE OF
THE P ARRANGEMENT

THE P ARRANGEMENT
DELANEY

Sitting on the floor in my old bathroom and watching my son play in the bathtub felt surreal. Truthfully, this whole night had been surreal. I had lived in this house, used this bathroom, slept in the bed out there for more years than my current home. It was supposed to be where my ex and I were going to raise our children. It was no wonder it felt surreal.

"I got the kitchen cleaned up, including Paxton's seat," Preston said, walking into the bathroom. He held up two articles of clothing. "Here are Pax's PJs." He set them on the counter and leaned against it.

"Oh, good. It's probably time for him to get out."

Our son yawned.

"Definitely time for him to get out," I corrected.

I stood, and without thinking, I opened up the linen closet and pulled out a towel like I'd done a million times before. As I closed the door, I wondered if I should have asked first, but at the same time, it seemed silly to ask when Paxton needed a towel and I knew where they were.

I mentally shrugged. It was too late now.

"Okay, buddy, it's time to get out."

Paxton looked up at me with all the confidence of a toddler. "No."

"Yes," I said, using a sterner voice.

He looked at his father and back at me. "No."

I counted to ten because I knew he was tired. Arguing with him never got me anywhere when he was sleepy, but it was hard to not show my frustration. I was exhausted too.

Preston pushed himself off the counter. "Paxton, it's time to get out."

He looked his father right in the eye. "No."

Preston and I exchanged glances, and I could tell he was thinking the same thing I was. *What the hell are we going to do with him?*

I had to purse my lips so I didn't laugh.

Being a single parent could be hard, and it was nice to know I wasn't alone, especially when it came to the same kid.

Facing our wayward child, I shrugged and said in my best nonchalant voice, "Okay, you have fun here." I hung up the towel on the rack. "I'm going to go read Daddy a bedtime story since you would rather stay in the tub."

Preston made a sound beside me, but when I turned to him, he was already acting for Paxton's benefit. "Ooh, I love bedtime stories." He rubbed his hands together. "Let me go grab a book."

"*No*." Paxton scrambled up. "I get story."

I pretended to not understand. "Does this mean you want to get out?"

"*Yes*." His little brow furrowed.

"Oh, okay."

I pulled the towel from the rack, and when Paxton spun around for me to wrap it around his back, Preston gave me a fist bump.

I had to hide my smile from Paxton when he turned back around. Thankfully, he was too focused on getting out of the bathtub and putting his pajamas on to realize he wasn't the one who'd won.

His father and I walked him to his room.

"Okay, buddy, give Mommy a hug and kiss so you can lie down."

I still hadn't talked to Preston about switching weekends, but Paxton needed to go to bed. And I was beginning to think it would be easier to take my sister up on her offer to watch him. Preston and I had gotten along tonight. I didn't want to ruin that by asking for a favor.

Paxton frowned. "Read story, Mommy." Unlike in the tub, his voice was sad and confused.

"Daddy's going to read you a story." I got down on my haunches and took his hands. "Mommy's going to read you a story when I see you on Sunday."

He let go of my hands and wrapped his little arms

around my neck. "No, Mommy. Read story to me and Daddy."

Oh man. How was I supposed to resist him when he was being so adorable?

Wrapping my arms around him, I hugged him tight. "Mommy—"

"Will read a story to both of us. And then Daddy will read a story to you and Mommy," Preston said.

I looked up at him and mouthed, *Are you sure?*

He smiled and nodded.

"Did you hear that?" I said to Paxton. "You get two stories."

"Yay!" He let me go and ran over to his full-size bed. It looked enormous around him, but he'd grow into it someday.

He patted the mattress on one side of him. "Mommy lay here." And then he patted the other side. "Daddy lay here."

Relief hit me because I hadn't even thought about him possibly suggesting that his father and I lie down next to each other. I wouldn't have wanted another argument with Paxton, but I also didn't know if I could have lain on a bed beside my ex without needing a long therapy session after.

Preston and I got on the bed with our son, and he handed me a book.

"We've been reading this one a lot lately."

I nodded and read the title. "Does this work, Pax?"

He nodded, and I began to read.

I hoped that before I was finished, Paxton would fall

asleep. Although he was clearly tired, when I closed the book, he was still awake.

"Daddy's turn."

So, while Preston found something else to read, I settled in next to Paxton. I always missed him when he was with his dad, so I made sure to enjoy these last few minutes together.

Preston started the second book, and I could feel myself nodding off toward the end, but before I knew it, he said the words, *"The End."*

I lifted my gaze to see him smiling down at our son, the love showing clearly from his eyes.

It made my heart clench.

"He's out."

"Oh, good." My voice came out tighter than I'd wanted it to. I cleared my throat and carefully stood. "That's our cue to leave."

It was also my cue to leave the house.

I kissed Paxton on the forehead and brushed my hand over his head. "I'll see you in a couple of days, sweetheart," I whispered.

Reluctantly, I pulled away and rounded his bed toward the half-closed bedroom door as Preston turned off the lamp next to the bed. While the sun was going down and there was a bit of light peeking from underneath the blinds and curtain, it was not enough to show the toy in my path. Of course, I tripped.

More afraid of waking Paxton than getting hurt if I crashed into something, I reached for the nearest thing.

My ex-husband.

Preston caught me before I crashed into the bed, and we both froze. With a quick look to see if our son was still sleeping, he kicked the truck out of the way, and we hurried out the door, silently laughing the whole way.

"Holy crap, that was close," I told him when we slipped out of the room.

Preston reached behind me to close the door and grinned. "I thought for sure you were going down."

I put my palms on his chest. "Thanks for saving me." My heart was racing from my near fall.

A click sounded behind me, and Preston shifted his eyes to my hands as his smile slowly slipped from his face.

When he lifted his chin, I wasn't prepared to see the heat in them, and my heart started pounding for a whole other reason.

As if we shared a thought, our mouths crashed together as we wrapped our arms around each other. I parted my lips, and Preston plunged his tongue inside. I groaned at the taste of him. It was familiar and welcoming in a way I hadn't felt in way too long.

And that was what lifted the sexual cloud that had descended on my brain.

I needed to stop this before I got hurt, and without a second thought, I slipped from his arms and bolted down the stairs.

ABOUT THE AUTHOR

R.L. Kenderson is two best friends writing under one name.

Renae has always loved reading, and in third grade, she wrote her first poem where she learned she might have a knack for this writing thing. Lara remembers sneaking her grandmother's Harlequin novels when she was probably too young to be reading them, and since then, she knew she wanted to write her own.

When they met in college, they bonded over their love of reading and the TV show *Charmed*. What really spiced up their friendship was when Lara introduced Renae to romance novels. When they discovered their first vampire romance, they knew there would always be a special place in their hearts for paranormal romance. After being unable to find certain storylines and characteristics they wanted to read about in the hundreds of books they consumed, they decided to write their own.

One lives in the Minneapolis-St. Paul area and the other in the Kansas City area where they both work in the medical field during the day and a sexy author by night. They communicate through phone, email, and whole lot of messaging.

You can find them at http://www.rlkenderson.com, Facebook, Instagram, TikTok, and Goodreads. Join their reader group! Or you can email them at rlkenderson@ rlkenderson.com, or sign up for their newsletter. They always love hearing from their readers.

Printed in Great Britain
by Amazon